The Search for the Snow Leopard

Joe glanced down, finding himself no more than two stories off the ground. Not so bad, Joe thought. If I can't pull myself up, I'll just drop down.

But Joe changed his mind when he saw the lions directly below, gazing up at him. There were several sleek beige lionesses and a single male. Everything about the male—his broad nose, his steady eyes, the majestic mane of hair circling his face—proclaimed authority.

Chet might not think the lion is king of the jungle, Joe thought, but he looks pretty terrifying from this angle.

The monorail screeched to a stop as Joe felt his precious grip on the door slip. His palms were sweating like crazy. He slipped again, struggling to keep his sweaty fingers on the door.

"Help!" he screamed.

Below him, the male lion opened up his mouth and gave a thunderous roar!

The Hardy Boys Mystery Stories

Available from ALADDIN Paperbacks

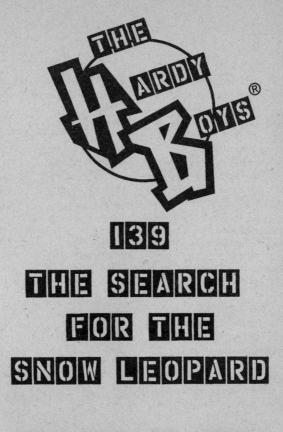

139

THE SEARCH FOR THE SNOW LEOPARD

FRANKLIN W. DIXON

Aladdin Paperbacks
New York   London   Toronto   Sydney   Singapore

First Aladdin Paperbacks edition June 2002
First Minstrel edition August 1996

Copyright © 1996 by Simon & Schuster, Inc.
Produced by Mega-Books, Inc.

ALADDIN PAPERBACKS
An imprint of Simon & Schuster
Children's Publishing Division
1230 Avenue of the Americas
New York, NY 10020

Printed in the United States of America

20 19 18 17 16 15

THE HARDY BOYS and THE HARDY BOYS MYSTERY STORIES are trademarks of Simon & Schuster, Inc.

ISBN-13: 978-0-671-50525-7
ISBN-10: 0-671-50525-4
0412 OFF

Contents

1 An Honored Guest

"Chet has finally met his match," Frank Hardy told his brother, Joe.

"That's right," Joe agreed. "That elephant probably eats as much as he does."

The brothers roared with laughter. They were leaning against a railing at the Bayport Zoo, watching a five-ton elephant. At the moment the elephant wasn't eating, he was getting a manicure. As the gray elephant obediently held up one of its massive front feet, a zookeeper filed the toenails with a rasp. Standing beside the elephant was Frank and Joe's best friend, Chet Morton.

"I heard that," Chet called to the Hardys. Chet was wearing a T-shirt that read Zoo Intern. Every summer the zoo took on a group of student volunteers to help out and learn about the animals in the process. Chet had signed up and was now in his final month at the zoo.

"Do they also put red polish on his nails?" Joe cracked.

"Only for special occasions," Frank replied.

The Hardys watched the beauty treatment, and Frank marveled at the elephant's gargantuan size and rough bristly hide. He thought the animal resembled a gigantic gray tank with big floppy ears.

At eighteen, Frank Hardy was a year older and an inch taller than his brother. He had dark hair, brown eyes, and was the more logical of the two Hardys. Joe had blond hair, blue eyes, and tended to be a bit hotheaded. Both Hardys were wearing their official summer vacation uniforms—T-shirts, cutoffs, and sneakers.

When the manicure was over, the elephant scooped at the ground with its long trunk.

"Watch out!" the keeper cried. Chet and the keeper ducked for cover as the elephant tossed its trunk upward and gave itself an explosive shower of dirt and dust.

"Yeccch," Chet cried, brushing dirt from his light brown hair.

As the Hardys chuckled, Chet and the keeper went inside a barnlike structure. A few moments later Chet met the Hardys on the other side of the railing. Chet was now carrying a big bag of popcorn.

"By the way, Chet, does the elephant share your fondness for junk food?" Joe asked.

"Hey, you'd better not laugh at the elephant," Chet retorted. "The truth is, the elephant is the real king of the jungle. He can lick a lion any day of the week. All he has to do is step on him."

"How do you know he won't step on you?" Frank asked, not completely in jest.

"Oh, Hero and I are old friends," Chet said, glancing back at the elephant. "In fact, she's my favorite animal at the zoo. But we need to get over to the cat compound. There's a really big event starting in about ten minutes. A snow leopard is making her debut."

Chet led the Hardys through the zoo grounds. Wide, paved walkways wound through the sprawling park. Frank admired the zoo's clever design: the animal habitats blended perfectly with the trees and shrubbery.

"Great day to be at the zoo," Joe said, stretching his arms. The sky was bright blue and the sun felt pleasantly warm.

"We're not the only ones who think so," Frank said, noticing the large number of people wandering through the grounds.

"In the United States, more people visit zoos in one year," Chet said, popping a kernel of popcorn in his mouth, "than go to all the professional sporting events put together."

"Really?" Joe said, surprised.

3

Chet nodded. "They're really popular."

Soon the boys came to another "enclosure," this one consisting of trampled muddy grass and an even muddier pond.

"Chet, you'd better clean that water," Frank teased, leaning on a railing.

"It's supposed to look like African swampland," Chet said. "Zoos try hard to make the animals' living quarters resemble their natural habitats," he explained.

Joe suddenly spotted a giant boulder moving in the pond. "Hey," he cried. "Look at that rock!" Then he realized the "boulder" was really a hippopotamus. With a low moaning sound, the huge animal opened its mouth, revealing teeth the size of human fingers.

"Whoa, check out the teeth," Frank said. "They're enormous."

"I bet he's a handful," Joe commented.

"I'll put it this way," Chet said with a grin. "When he goes to the bathroom, you don't want to be in the neighborhood."

"I don't even want to be in the same city!" Joe joked.

The boys continued their journey, soon passing a sign that read Cat Compound. They stopped when they came to another enclosure, this one filled with the leafy plants and tall thin trees of the Asian jungle. Joe noticed two Bengal tigers lounging in the shade of a tree.

As with the other enclosures, there was a railing

to keep the public back. Several feet beyond the rail, a deep concrete "moat" with no water ran around the enclosure.

"Most of the displays have dry moats like that," Chet explained. "The moat forms a barrier the animal can't get past."

"Nice solution," Frank observed. "No cage, but the animal can't get to the general public."

"Good thing, too," Joe said, watching the sleek orange tigers with their black stripes. The tigers seemed lazy now, but Joe knew they could be killing machines.

For a moment Frank imagined he was deep in the heart of a steamy jungle, watching the tigers from behind the camouflage of some trees.

The boys resumed walking and soon passed an enclosure decorated with the rocky crags and sand of the American Southwest. Blending into the scenery, two light brown mountain cougars lay asleep on the rocks.

"The rocks are actually fake," Chet explained. "They're made from a synthetic substance called gunite. Most of the rocks and caves and trees in the zoo exhibits are made from it. All these things help create the illusion of being in the animals' homeland."

"What's happening up there?" Joe pointed to an enclosure where a large crowd had gathered. People buzzed with excitement, their cameras ready for action. Some of the adults had small children perched on their shoulders.

This enclosure was steeply banked like a mountainside, and even though it was summer, there were patches of snow on the ground.

"This area is designed to resemble the Himalayan mountains," Chet explained. "That's where the snow leopard comes from. By the way, the snow is also fake."

"Must be a big deal—I see some members of the press," Joe said, scanning the crowd. Then he noticed a man and a woman, each holding up a sign. One sign read Zoos Are Inhuman! The other sign read Set the Animals Free!

I wonder what that's about, Joe thought.

Near the snow leopard enclosure, a man stood at a podium. He had on a shirt and tie, and his handsome, tanned face was topped with blond hair. Joe guessed he was in his early forties.

"Welcome to the Bayport Zoo," the blond man announced. "My name is Randy Chase, and I'm the zoo director. Today is a great day for the zoo because today we debut our first snow leopard. The leopard is a gift from a very special young lady. Her name is Salamaji and she is a princess. That's right, an authentic princess from the country of Rashipah. Your Highness, why don't you explain why you're giving us this beautiful and very rare animal."

Frank watched a girl about his own age step up to the podium. The girl was quite beautiful, her skin a deep tan color. She had long black hair and eyes equally dark.

Frank knew the long piece of purple fabric wrapped around her body was called a sari.

"Hello." The princess spoke in a clear voice. "My name is Salamaji and I come from Rashipah. This is a very tiny country just north of India. Several years ago I was given a snow leopard cub as a gift. I named her Emi, which means 'friend' in my country, and she has been a beloved pet to me."

The crowd listened closely as she explained that she'd come to Bayport University to study.

"I wanted Emi to stay close to me," the princess went on with a smile. "But since they do not allow leopards in my dormitory, I decided to give her as a present to the Bayport Zoo."

The crowd laughed at her joke. Though the princess spoke English well, Frank could tell it was not her native language.

"I just arrived in Bayport two months ago," the princess continued, "but so far everyone has been very friendly to me. I sincerely hope that you will extend the same . . . what is the word . . . hospitality . . . to my snow leopard, Emi. Thank you very much."

As the crowd applauded, the princess stepped away from the podium, and Chase took her place.

"Before I introduce you to Emi," Randy Chase announced, "there is one more human I would like to introduce. He, too, has a special gift for us and I'll let him tell you about it. Please welcome a great naturalist and animal lover, Theodore K. Anglethorpe!"

Joe watched Theodore K. Anglethorpe step up to the podium. Anglethorpe was a big bear of a man with a rugged face and a mane of flowing white hair. He wore khakis and a safari shirt with epaulets on the shoulders. Joe thought Anglethorpe looked as if he could wrestle a lion, outsmart a fox, and charm an alligator all at the same time.

"Howdy," Anglethorpe said, waving to the crowd. "I'm one of those eccentric old millionaires you sometimes read about. Fortunately, I inherited my money so I never had to work much. This has given me plenty of time to pursue my passion for animals. I hunt them, study them, and even collect them."

"If he loves them so much, why does he hunt them?" Joe muttered.

"A lot of hunters are animal lovers," Frank pointed out. "Very often hunters help keep a species from overpopulating."

"You see," Anglethorpe continued, "I live on a small island away out on the bay, and I keep a menagerie of exotic animals out there. So one day a couple of months ago, I get a call from Mr. Chase asking if I happened to have a male snow leopard and, if so, would I lend him to the zoo for a while. Seems he was getting this female snow leopard and he was looking to find a nice husband for it."

Anglethorpe smiled and some people laughed.

"Well," Anglethorpe continued, "I do have a male snow leopard. And in a few weeks I'm going to bring my leopard out here and we'll see what

8

happens. We hope they'll get along just fine and we'll have a few more snow leopards in the world."

The crowd applauded as Anglethorpe left the podium and Chase returned to it.

"And now for the guest of honor," Chase proclaimed. "I'll ask everybody not to cheer or make too much noise because we don't want to scare our new friend. People of Bayport, I give you Emi!"

As Chase made a signal at the enclosure, the crowd quieted and waited eagerly for the leopard's appearance. A moment passed. Nothing happened.

"Where is she?" Joe wondered.

"She's coming," Chet assured his friend.

A moment later, the snow leopard emerged from behind some gunite rocks at the rear of the enclosure.

Sounds of hushed awe came from the crowd, and Frank understood why. The snow leopard was an extraordinarily beautiful creature. She was slightly smaller than a tiger but moved with the slinky grace common to all felines. The leopard's luxurious fur was a pale, smoky gray color, dappled all over with black splotches.

"What a cool cat," Joe whispered as the leopard ambled effortlessly along the mountainside. There was a long piece of red fabric lying in the snow, and Emi walked over to sniff it.

"That's a sari that belongs to the princess," Chet whispered. "The scent of the princess helps the leopard feel more at home."

Joe noticed the princess standing at the railing,

9

fondly watching Emi. She wiped a tear from her eye.

A second later Joe heard screams in the near distance. He whipped his head around to see a handful of visitors running frantically toward the crowd. Joe could read the fear in their faces.

"Everybody run!" a teenage girl yelled as she ran by. "A tiger's escaped! A tiger's escaped!"

2 Do Tigers Eat People?

All around Frank, Joe, and Chet, people began to scream and flee. Cries of "Run!" and "Tiger!" and "Watch out!" pierced the peaceful afternoon.

Joe saw Randy Chase running in the direction where the tiger was supposed to be. Chase pulled a walkie-talkie from his belt and shouted into it.

"Frank, Chet!" Joe called. "Let's go!"

Joe raced after Chase with Frank and Chet following close behind. Visitors ran in the opposite direction, most shouting in sheer terror. As Joe ran past the mountain cougar exhibit, it occurred to him that most people run away from danger. For some reason, he was always running toward it!

Moments later, Joe stopped dead in his tracks. One of the Bengal tigers he had seen earlier was

11

standing on the walkway near its jungle enclosure. The reports were true. The tiger was definitely out!

Chase was standing a few yards away from the tiger. "Easy, boy," the zoo director said in low, soothing tones. "Everything is going to be just fine."

The tiger just stood there, gazing at Chase. Joe thought he seemed confused, uncertain where to go or what to do next.

The area was now vacated except for Chase, Chet, and the Hardys. Joe saw the other Bengal tiger was still in its jungle home, asleep beneath a tree.

"Can we help?" Frank asked Chase.

Chase glanced quickly at the boys, noticing Chet was a zoo intern. "Two of you can make sure people stay back," he instructed. "One of you can help me keep an eye on the tiger. Reinforcements should be here any second."

As Joe and Chet turned to keep people back, Joe spied one of the press photographers trotting toward the area. "Sorry," Joe called, running to stop the man. "You've got to stay back."

Meanwhile Frank inched over to Chase.

"Just talk to me," Chase told him. "The best thing to do is carry on a conversation like nothing is wrong."

"Okay," Frank said, keeping a careful eye on the escaped tiger. "Uh, let me ask you . . . Do tigers eat people?"

"Not usually," Chase replied. "They prefer something like gazelle. Isn't that right, boy?"

The tiger gave a low rumbling growl.

Though the tiger looked quite menacing, Frank noticed its whiskers and tail were a lot like those of a common house cat.

"Big cats don't often kill for sport either," Chase continued. "They're too lazy. They kill for food or to protect their territory. Now, if you went inside his space, I wouldn't give you much of a chance."

Suddenly the tiger fixed its yellowish eyes on Frank.

"Hi, there, boy," Frank said softly. Behind the tiger Frank could see a green zoo Jeep driving slowly along the walkway behind the tiger.

"Keep your eye contact with him," Chase whispered to Frank. "We don't want him to see what's happening."

"Remember," Frank told the tiger as convincingly as possible, "you guys don't like to eat people."

The Jeep stopped, and two men in light green zoo uniforms climbed out. One carried a rifle and the other had a three-foot-long copper tube.

"Stay very still," Chase advised. "They're going to shoot a few tranquilizer darts with a blowgun. On impact, the darts inject a drug that puts the animal out for about twenty minutes."

Frank saw the man with the copper tube creep up stealthily behind the tiger. The man put the tube to his mouth, took careful aim, and the next second a dart with an orange tassle on the end zoomed straight into the tiger's right flank.

The tiger snarled, and Frank glimpsed two razor-sharp fangs in the tiger's mouth.

Another dart hit the tiger's left flank.

"Arrrrrr!" the tiger growled ferociously. His eyes burned with rage as he lunged toward Frank.

Before Frank could react, the tiger's rear legs buckled and he slumped to the ground. Then the animal rolled back his head and closed his eyes.

"Whew!" Frank let out a sigh of relief.

Chase approached cautiously and touched the tiger on his side. "He's out cold."

The two men from the Jeep set a canvas stretcher beside the tiger, and Chase helped the men lift the drugged tiger onto it. Then the three men carried the tiger to the Jeep, and moments later the vehicle drove off.

A crowd of visitors and zoo employees had gathered to watch the excitement from a safe distance.

"Any idea what happened?" a reporter shouted, running up to Chase.

"No comment right now," Chase said, waving the man off. Then Chase turned to Chet and the Hardys. "Thanks for your help, boys. I shouldn't have put you at risk, but you were the only ones around."

"Don't mention it," Chet told Chase. "All in the line of duty. And these guys"—Chet jerked a

14

thumb in the Hardys' direction—"have faced down tougher foes than a Bengal tiger."

"Is that right?" Chase said with a laugh. Frank could tell Chase thought that Chet was joking.

"Frank, Joe, I'll see you later," Chet called to his friends. "I've got an appointment with a camel who needs his hump scrubbed."

As Chet ran off, the Hardys followed Chase to the railing of the tiger enclosure. The other Bengal was still sleeping peacefully.

Frank studied the tigers' habitat. "So that's how he escaped," he remarked a few seconds later. A large tree limb had fallen across the moat, creating a bridge. The tiger had probably walked across it, then easily jumped the railing.

Chase had also spotted the fallen limb. "Let's clear this branch so the other tiger can't get out!" he called. Immediately two zoo employees rushed over to knock the limb into the moat with a long pole.

Joe kneeled down near the moat to get a better look at the fallen limb. A second later, he glanced at Frank. His older brother was thinking the same thing.

"This was no accident," Frank said grimly.

Chase looked startled. "What?"

"Look at this." Joe pointed to the nearest end of the limb. "This branch was sawed partway through. And if you look at the far end of the limb, you'll notice there's a rope attached to it."

"Someone could have sawed that limb last night or even several days ago," Frank commented. "Then attached the rope to it, letting the rope hang near the ground."

"When the culprit was ready," Joe added, "he just gave the rope a yank. He probably did it in the last half hour. He must have known most everybody was over at the snow leopard exhibit."

Chase was staring at the boys. "Are you guys detectives, or something?" he asked, clearly amazed by what he'd heard.

Frank and Joe exchanged a look. Then Frank gave a tiny nod.

"Actually, sir, yes, we are," Joe said. He quickly told Chase about some of the cases he and Frank had solved in and out of the Bayport area.

"I thought Chet was joking. Why don't you guys follow me to my office and we can talk," Chase told the Hardys.

"Any ideas on who might have done this?" Joe asked as Chase and the Hardys began walking.

"No," Chase replied. "And this isn't the first time something like this has happened. A month ago, a couple of monkeys escaped, and then, two weeks ago, a python got out. Why don't I show you?"

A slight detour brought Chase and the Hardys to the Japanese macaque enclosure. It was a rocky island with a few trees, surrounded by a moat that was actually filled with water. Joe watched a few of the macaques leap playfully across the rocks at great speed. They were monkeys with gray fur and little red faces that looked vaguely human.

"The monkeys would be able to get out," Chase said, pointing to the back of the island, "if it weren't for a section of hot-wire up there. Right by those trees."

"What's hot-wire?" Joe asked.

"It's hard to see it," Chase said, "but if the monkeys touch it they get a mild electrical shock. Anyway, a month ago, two of the monkeys escaped and we discovered someone had snipped the hot-wire."

Studying the enclosure, Frank noted the hot-wire was in a very high and hard-to-reach spot. Even with a ladder, it would be tough to get to.

A few minutes later, Chase led the Hardys to a handsome tan brick building not far away. "This is the back of the reptile house," Chase explained. "Inside, we keep the reptiles in small display rooms with protective glass in front."

"Sounds like a good idea," Joe said, grinning. He gave a mock shiver. "That's how I like snakes— behind protective glass."

"Now look up there at that air vent." Chase pointed to a metal air vent just above a drainpipe. "All the display cases are temperature controlled, and we have vents running around the building's exterior. Well, someone dislodged that vent and also the vent leading into a python's case."

"So the python slithered its way through an air duct and down the drainpipe," Frank guessed.

"Two weeks ago I got a call on my walkie-talkie saying there was a python slithering along the sidewalk," Chase went on. "The snake isn't poisonous, but it sure scared some folks."

"But today's breakout *was* really dangerous," Joe commented. "Letting a Bengal tiger out of its habitat isn't just a little prank."

Chase nodded. "You're absolutely right."

"In each case," Frank added thoughtfully, "the actual sabotage must have been done during off hours. Otherwise, the culprit would have been seen. So maybe he saved the finishing touch for the next day, to be sure the animal's escape would occur during public hours."

"We have security guards patrolling the grounds during off hours," Chase explained. "But it's not impossible for someone to sneak onto the grounds. In fact, it happens sometimes."

"Or the culprit could be one of the security guards," Joe pointed out.

"Right." Chase sighed wearily. "That's the problem. It could be practically anybody. And neither I nor the police have any idea who it is."

Next, Chase led the Hardys to Zoo Plaza, a paved area surrounded by an array of flowers and sculpted shrubbery. In the center of the plaza was a fountain, where water shot from the mouths of marble seals.

"My office is in the administration building," Chase said, nodding toward another tan brick structure. Joe noticed a police car parked nearby.

"I'm going to meet with my head of security and the police," Chase went on. "Would you care to join us? Maybe you two can help us crack this case."

"Count us in," Frank stated.

"But we'll skip the meeting," Joe said. "There's something I'd like to check right away. Do you know anything about those two protesters I saw at the snow leopard debut?"

"Oh, that's Jeff and Janet Kellerman," Chase explained. "They're animal-rights activists. They showed up in town a few months ago, and sometimes they protest out here. The zoo is city property so as long as they're peaceful, we can't toss them out. I never suspected the Kellermans of these crimes, but then again they sure don't like zoos."

The Hardys promised to check back with Chase later and went in search of the Kellermans. Within minutes, Frank and Joe found the protesters handing out pamphlets in the zoo parking lot. Their signs were now leaning against a lamppost.

Joe glanced at the sign that read Set the Animals Free! as Janet Kellerman stopped an elderly lady.

"The Bayport Zoo is not fair to animals," Janet said, handing the woman a pamphlet. "Read this before you go inside."

"Please read this before you enter," Jeff Kellerman said, giving a teenage couple a pamphlet.

Chase was right, Joe thought. These people *hate* zoos.

Frank and Joe kept their distance from the Kellermans. They wanted to watch the protesters in action. Jeff had a beard and long brown hair tied in a ponytail, and Janet had short, blond hair. They were both slender and athletic, and Frank guessed they were in their mid-thirties. Both protesters wore T-shirts with the letters *ARF* printed on them.

Soon a young man with a camera around his neck walked up to the Kellermans. "Why do you guys have to make trouble at the zoo?" the man asked. "The zoo takes great care of its animals."

"Believe me," Janet told the man, "the animals can take much better care of themselves in the wild. And if you want to see them, that's where you should go. It's not fair to keep them trapped in a zoo."

"Well, maybe I can't afford to travel all over the world," the man with the camera argued.

"But you can afford a real alligator-skin belt," Jeff Kellerman said, pointing to the man's belt. "And real leather shoes made from a cow's precious hide."

Joe saw a few people turn to watch the argument.

"You guys are fanatics," the man with the camera said, giving Jeff a disgusted look. "You're just making trouble for the sake of making trouble."

"Mister," Jeff growled back, "it's not the animals who belong in cages. It's people like you!"

"You can't talk to me like that," the man said.

"Oh, yeah?" Then Jeff gave him a rough shove in the chest.

"Hey!" the man cried.

Is this guy, Jeff, always so hotheaded? Frank thought.

But Frank didn't have time to wonder about Jeff's temper for much longer. Jeff and the man with the camera started circling each other angrily, then Jeff cocked a fist.

If Frank didn't do something—and do it soon— Jeff Kellerman would smash the man in the face!

3 Ambushed

"Wait," Frank called, rushing to catch hold of Kellerman's arm. Joe was right behind him. "You're not helping your cause any by belting this guy."

Jeff Kellerman turned to Frank, a furious expression on his face.

"He's right," Janet Kellerman appealed to her husband. "Let this creep go, Jeff. I mean it."

Jeff lowered his clenched fist.

"Fanatics!" the man with the camera scowled. "You guys are real nuts. Now, if you'll excuse me, I am going to have myself a nice visit at the zoo." The man turned and stomped toward a ticket hut with a thatched roof.

"Thanks for stopping me, kid," Jeff told Frank. "I get a little carried away sometimes."

"I guess you feel pretty strongly about your cause," Frank said.

"Somebody has to." Jeff handed Frank a pamphlet. "My wife and I run a small organization called ARF. It stands for Animal Rights Force. We protect the civil rights of animals."

"I didn't know animals had civil rights," Joe said, wondering if these guys really were nuts.

"They don't," Janet replied sharply. "But they should. Read our literature when you get a chance."

"We will," Frank said, glancing at the pamphlet.

"Come on, honey," Janet said, taking her husband's arm. "We've done enough protesting for one day. Let's buy some fresh vegetables and go home."

Joe watched the Kellermans pick up their signs and walk toward a nearby bus stop. "What do you think of them?" he asked Frank.

"I think we should keep an eye on them," Frank said. "They've certainly got a motive for creating trouble at the zoo. But for now, let's hang around here."

Joe readily agreed. "Maybe we can cruise around the zoo and look for clues," he said. "Whoever's sabotaging the animals' exhibits has probably left behind some kind of evidence."

For the next hour Frank and Joe wandered around the spacious zoo, keeping their eyes peeled for anything suspicious. Joe couldn't help noticing again how well the grounds were kept—the park was beautiful.

23

By the time they had covered most of the zoo, they hadn't spotted anything odd, except for an aardvark sniffing at the dirt with its snout.

"Let's talk with Chet again," Frank suggested finally. "Maybe he's done brushing the camel's teeth."

"I think it was the camel's hump." Joe grinned.

"Whatever," Frank replied.

The Hardys cut through the African plains, where a monorail traveled over their heads.

"Chet says that's a pretty cool ride," Joe told Frank. "Maybe we can check it out."

Frank nodded. "Definitely. As soon as we get this case solved."

The Hardys caught up with Chet back at the snow leopard enclosure, where a sizable crowd was still gathered. To their amazement, Chet wasn't with an animal, but instead he was talking with Salamaji—the beautiful princess of Rashipah.

"Hi, guys," Chet called. "Salamaji, I'd like you to meet my two best buds, Frank and Joe Hardy."

"Buds?" Salamaji said with a confused expression. "Do you mean like flower buds?"

"Uh, no." Chet snickered. "'Buds' is short for buddies, which is, uh . . ."

"Friends," Salamaji said, smoothing her purple sari. "I understand now."

"It's an honor to meet you," Frank said.

"Yeah, uh, same here," Joe stammered. Unsure what to do when meeting a princess, he gave a little bow.

24

"No bowing necessary," Salamaji said warmly. Then she turned to Chet. "May I try one of those?" She pointed to the box of Cracker Jack candied popcorn in his hand.

"Oh, sure," Chet said.

"I'm afraid I've never heard of Rashipah," Frank admitted to the princess.

"Neither have most people," Salamaji said, tasting a Cracker Jack. "That's because it is very tiny and very far away. Mmmm, these are quite good."

"Is your father the king there?" Frank asked.

"Yes." Salamaji nodded. "But my father is mostly a symbolic leader. Rashipah is a democracy now, but the people like having a royal family around for parades and postage stamps and so forth."

Frank heard laughter and turned to see two kids playing tag in the grass. Then Frank noticed something else. Off in the distance a teenage boy was standing beneath a large oak tree.

The odd thing was, the boy seemed to be staring straight at Frank. Or maybe, Frank realized a second later, he was staring at Salamaji. Frank didn't blame him—it wasn't often a genuine princess visited Bayport!

"Why did you choose Bayport University?" Chet was asking.

"All over the world, people are curious about the United States," Salamaji explained. "And a cousin of mine had come to Bayport University, and she liked it very much. I start my freshman year in the fall, but I'm taking a few summer school courses

25

right now to . . . what's the phrase . . . get ahead. Chet, may I try another Cracker Jack?"

Suddenly, Frank heard a high-pitched yowling sound. He spun around to see where it came from.

"That's just Emi," Salamaji said, indicating the enclosure. Beyond the railing and past the moat, Emi was gazing at Salamaji with her icy green eyes. Frank noticed the leopard had one paw protectively wrapped around the red sari that had been left in her enclosure. "Snow leopards are the only animals that make that particular sound," Salamaji went on.

"What does she want?" Chet asked.

"Oh, she just wants my attention," Salamaji said with a smile. "She gets jealous sometimes." Then Salamaji called the words *"Gaba kima nu"* to the leopard, who grunted back.

Joe listened in amazement. It was as if the two of them were having a real conversation!

"Do snow leopards live in your country?" Joe asked, admiring Emi's gorgeous coat of spotted fur.

"Close by," Salamaji explained. "They live in the Himalayan mountain range, which extends from India to China. They stay very high up in the snowy region, way above all people and other animals. The snow leopard is a very private creature. They are like me in that respect."

Frank turned and saw the boy was still staring in their direction. Though the boy was dressed like an American, Frank noticed he had the same dark hair and skin color as Salamaji.

26

Frank's instincts went on alert. I don't like the way that guy is staring at the princess, he thought.

"In Rashipah, did Emi stay at your house?" Chet asked.

"Every night she slept at the foot of my bed," Salamaji replied. "But she was getting too big to be a house pet. I would have liked to release her back into the wild, but once an animal has been domesticated, it is hard to do that. She wouldn't know how to fend for herself in the mountains. So I gave her to the Bayport Zoo instead. But first thing every morning I come to visit her."

Salamaji gave Emi a loving gaze, and the snow leopard nuzzled her nose against the sari. Then the princess blew Emi a kiss. Joe could tell there was a deep bond between the pair.

"Why don't we take a stroll?" Salamaji abruptly turned away from the leopard. "It's such a beautiful afternoon. I just hope we don't come across a runaway rhinoceros."

Chet laughed so hard at this that Joe checked to make sure his friend wasn't choking on a Cracker Jack. Meanwhile, Frank glanced back at the oak tree and was relieved to see that the mysterious boy was gone.

The princess and the three friends walked along a shady walkway.

"Speaking of runaway animals," Joe began, "Chet, did you know there have been two other escapes at the zoo?"

"Yeah," Chet answered. "I didn't say anything

before because Mr. Chase didn't want everyone knowing about it."

"It's pretty obvious those escapes weren't accidental," Joe remarked. "Somebody is helping those animals to get away. The question is, who and why?"

"Fortunately, there haven't been any injuries so far," Frank added. "But if the escapes continue, somebody is bound to be hurt."

"Well, here we go," Chet announced. "Another case for the brave Hardy brothers." Chet leaned toward Salamaji and whispered, "These guys may not look like much, but they're actually detectives. And sometimes when they get stumped, they call on me for expert advice."

"Detectives?" Salamaji raised her eyebrows. "Truly? How exciting!"

"Why don't you announce it to the whole world?" Joe mumbled.

"I will keep your secret," Salamaji promised.

"Maybe you can help us now," Frank told Chet as the four of them crossed a little bridge that ran over a pond. "You've been working at the zoo for a few months. Have you noticed anything unusual?"

"I can't think of anything offhand," Chet said as the group stopped to watch the ducks and swans floating on the surface of the pond.

"Have you met any zoo employees who seem unhappy about anything?" Joe asked him.

Chet kept staring at the swan. "Dr. Godfrey," he said suddenly. "She's the primate curator."

"I know they have curators at museums," Frank said as the group resumed walking, "but what does a curator do at a zoo?"

"Well, keepers are the ones who take care of the animals," Chet explained. "And curators are the ones who oversee the management of a certain type of species. For example, Dr. Godfrey oversees all of the primates. That includes all the monkeys and apes."

"What makes you think she's unhappy?" Frank asked.

"She's famous for her research on chimpanzees," Chet said. "Anyway, one day I was in her lab and she was complaining how the zoo's board of trustees wanted to spend all this money on a special exhibit."

"What's wrong with that?" Frank wondered.

"She was planning to do some field research on chimps," Chet said, giving his elephant buddy, Hero, a wave. "But the zoo board suddenly decided to yank her funding and put it toward a new exhibit. I was there the day she heard about it, and she was plenty mad. She was even throwing files around."

"This is so interesting!" Salamaji exclaimed. "Just like American television."

"When was this incident?" Joe asked.

"About a month ago," Chet answered.

"A month ago," Frank said, stopping to think. "Wasn't that when the first animal escape happened?"

Chet nodded.

29

"Maybe we should pay this Dr. Godfrey a visit," Joe suggested. "The primate lady is already sounding like a prime sus——"

"Ow!" Frank exclaimed as something pounded his shoulder. "What just hit me?"

"I didn't see anything," Joe said, glancing all around. "Are you sure you were hit?"

"Of course I'm sure," Frank said, rubbing his shoulder. "You think I would just make it up?"

"Ow!" Joe jumped. "Something just hit me in the back!" An object bounced off his shoulder and rolled under some bushes.

"Duck for cover!" Frank yelled as his eyes flashed to the trees overhead. "I think we're being ambushed!"

4 Ape Avenue

"Watch the princess!" Joe shouted at Chet.

The princess's eyes were wide with fright. She threw herself onto the ground and covered her head with her hands.

Frank scanned the ground.

"Look," he said a second later. He scooped an apple off the ground and held it out to Joe. "I think this is what hit us!"

But Joe was staring at Chet. Instead of protecting the princess, Chet doubled over with laughter.

"What's so funny?" Frank demanded.

"It's not the princess they're after," Chet said between guffaws. "It's you guys!"

"What do you mean?" Joe demanded.

"The . . . uh . . . person who was throwing those apples," Chet cried in glee. "It was Hero!"

31

"Who?" Frank and Joe said together.

"Hero," Chet said, pointing to the nearby elephant enclosure. "She loves to throw things with her trunk. We try to keep throwable objects away from her, but sometimes visitors toss in apples and things."

Frank turned to see the enormous gray elephant, who was standing about thirty yards away. The elephant was looking Frank's way, and beneath her trunk, Frank could swear the animal was smiling.

"She was probably getting back at you fellows for laughing at her during her manicure," Chet remarked. "Remember, an elephant never forgets."

Salamaji stood up and brushed off her sari. "Are you boys all right?" she asked, trying not to smile herself.

"Yeah, fine," Joe muttered. "I just feel a little stupid. Chet, where might we find this famous Dr. Godfrey?"

"She's usually in her lab, just off Ape Avenue," Chet answered. "But she's usually really busy."

"Then we'd better take you to make introductions," Frank told Chet.

"Uh, sorry," Chet apologized. "I promised Salamaji I would show her the aviary. That's where they keep the birds. They have the most beautiful kookaburra you've ever set eyes on."

Salamaji smiled sweetly at Chet. Frank and Joe exchanged a puzzled look, then the Hardys set off to continue their investigation alone.

"I think Chet's gone cuckoo for the princess,"

Frank said as the brothers walked through the grounds.

"She seems to like him, too," Joe remarked.

"Why don't we stop by Randy Chase's office," Frank suggested. "We can have him set up an appointment with Dr. Godfrey."

"Good idea," Joe replied.

The Hardys quickly explained to Randy Chase that they wanted to talk to Dr. Godfrey. Frank also told him that they didn't want Dr. Godfrey to know they were looking into the case.

"You don't suspect Sara Godfrey?" Chase looked shocked.

Joe shrugged. "At this point we don't suspect anybody. But it would be better to have a cover."

Finally Chase put through the call and told Dr. Godfrey he was sending over some special "friends of the zoo."

Moments later Frank and Joe strolled past a sign that read Ape Avenue. They entered a building and walked along a corridor.

"It's King Kong's family," Joe suddenly joked. "Check out the gorillas."

Frank turned to see a group of gorillas separated from the public by a railing and then by clear fiberglass bars.

"They're actually very gentle," Frank told Joe. "Nothing like King Kong. See that adult gorilla picking straw off the baby?"

"You never did that for me when I was little," Joe said, grinning.

"And I wouldn't do it for you now," Frank shot back. "Come on. We'll be late for our appointment with Sara Godfrey."

A few minutes later, the Hardys came to a door marked Research Lab. After Joe knocked, the door buzzed open, and Frank and Joe stepped into a large room brightly lit by an overhead skylight. The room was divided in half by a wall of clear bars, like those on the gorilla enclosure. The near half of the room was filled with charts, graphs, books, video and sound equipment, a desk, and a few chairs.

Dr. Sara Godfrey was seated in a chair with a small chimpanzee in her lap. She was feeding him milk from a baby bottle.

The Hardys introduced themselves and she gestured for them to sit down. "So, you boys are interested in chimps?" she asked.

"Oh, we're just ape about them," Joe joked.

Dr. Godfrey smiled. She had a friendly face and gray hair pulled back into a bun. She wore a white lab coat, and Frank guessed she was at least fifty.

"Teri, would you release the cage lock?" Dr. Godfrey called to someone in an adjoining office. Then the scientist stood with the chimp and walked to the bars.

The other half of the room, beyond the clear bars, was considerably less businesslike. There was a fake tree, complete with sprawling limbs, green leaves, and a tire that hung from a rope. A big toy chest, rocking horse, and television set sat on the floor.

One chimp was perched in the tire, while another one pushed it, as if it were a playground swing. These two chimps were a bit larger than the baby, and obviously having a wonderful time.

Not a bad life, Joe mused.

"Okay," Teri yelled back to Dr. Godfrey. A second later, Frank heard a clicking sound, and Dr. Godfrey pushed open a door in the bars.

"There you go." Dr. Godfrey set the small chimp down in the barred area. Immediately the chimp scampered into the tree and started swinging from the limbs with the skill of an Olympic gymnast.

Frank and Joe walked over to the chimp area to watch them more closely. Each of the chimps stole a curious glance at the Hardys as they went about their play.

"These are my friends," Dr. Godfrey announced proudly. "Wendy, John, and the baby, Michael. They're all young, born in Africa. Their mother died and I was able to bring them here. You'll notice I've named them after characters in *Peter Pan.*"

"What sort of research are you doing with them?" Frank asked.

"Chimpanzees are the closest relatives to humans," Dr. Godfrey explained. "They share ninety-nine percent of their genetic makeup with us. My experiments are to determine just how similar they are to human beings."

"They sure look human!" Joe exclaimed. The chimps' hairy brownish black bodies were about

35

the size of a five-year-old child. And their facial features registered all sorts of human expressions. Right now they mostly looked curious about the visitors.

"In what ways are the chimps similar to humans?" Frank asked.

"We're discovering that chimps have many traits that used to be considered exclusively human," Dr. Godfrey revealed. "For example, chimps have distinctive personalities, emotions, imaginations; they can use tools; they can even speak."

"They can speak?" Joe was astonished.

"They sure can." Dr. Godfrey nodded. "They can't vocalize human words, but I've taught them sign language. The same kind used by hearing-impaired people. I'll demonstrate.

"John," Dr. Godfrey called. The chimp in the tire jumped down and walked on all fours to the bars. As Dr. Godfrey made a series of hand signals, the chimp watched with inquisitive brown eyes.

"I told him you two were 'zoo friends,'" Dr. Godfrey said. "They understand that 'zoo friends' means people who contribute money to the zoo. They don't fully understand the meaning of money, but they know it is important to us."

Then John made a series of hand signals. His nimble black fingers looked just like human fingers.

"What did he say?" Frank asked.

"'I like zoo friends,'" Dr. Godfrey translated.

Then John stuck a hand through the bars, palm up, as if he wanted something.

"I think he wants money," Joe said, laughing.

Joe pulled out his pockets to show he did not have any money in them. John shrugged, then turned his hand sideways as if he wanted to shake hands with Joe. Smiling, Joe walked up to the bars.

"Don't shake hands with him!" Dr. Godfrey warned.

Joe halted. "Why not?"

"He might break your arm," Dr. Godfrey explained. "Chimps are much stronger than we are, and their play can turn very dangerous. I know they look cute and adorable, but make no mistake, a chimpanzee can injure—and even kill—a person."

Suddenly, John signed something with his hand.

"What did he say?" Joe asked.

"He said, 'John no hurt person,'" Dr. Godfrey translated. "The truth is they've learned to understand a lot of spoken language, too. They're tremendously intelligent, and they can pick up almost anything." The scientist laughed ruefully. "And I mean almost anything."

John scampered to the toy chest and pulled out a long piece of wood. Wendy also went to the chest and pulled out a hammer and box of nails. To Joe's amazement, Wendy began hammering nails as John held the wood steady. Little Michael, still in the tree, clapped happily with approval.

"They could probably build a house if you taught them how," Joe observed.

"Probably," Dr. Godfrey agreed.

Learning about the chimps and watching them

37

was so interesting that Frank felt as if he could stay here all day. But he knew they'd better get back to the case. "Where does your research funding come from?" he asked the scientist.

"From the zoo," Dr. Godfrey told him. A dark cloud seemed to cross her face. "They were planning to send me and an assistant to Tanzania to do some field research. That's an African country with the largest chimpanzee population in the world. But the project's funding was suddenly cut off."

Joe noticed the chimps stopped their activity to watch the conversation.

"By whom?" Frank asked, trying not to sound as interested as he felt.

"By the zoo's board of trustees," Dr. Godfrey snapped. "They decided to take my funding money and put it toward a simulated South American rainforest they want to build here in the zoo."

Joe glanced at the chimps. How strange, he thought. The chimps had definitely sensed Dr. Godfrey's change in mood. As she spoke in angry tones, they each stuck out their lips and began making weird "ooh-ooh-ooh" noises.

"I have nothing against the rainforest project," Dr. Godfrey continued. "But I had been planning that trip for two years, and now it's canceled indefinitely. Plus I had to let an assistant go. They told me I could raise my own money independently, but, let me tell you, money for projects like mine certainly doesn't grow on trees!"

Wendy and John scampered into the tree, joining

little Michael. Their vocalizations were now high-pitched "eeh-eeh-eeh" sounds.

"Not only was that the most inconsiderate thing that's ever been done to me," Dr. Godfrey exclaimed, almost yelling, "but that research could have had some real meaning for everybody! Chimps and humans! It was an idiotic decision on the part of the zoo!"

The chimps started swinging from the tree limbs and screeching loudly. They were also showing their teeth, which Joe knew was a sign of rage.

"What's happening?" Frank glanced at the chimps in alarm.

"When I get mad about something, they get mad about it, too," Dr. Godfrey explained.

Joe could barely hear her, the din in the room was so loud. "Incredible," he called, holding his hands over his ears.

"All right, knock it off!" Dr. Godfrey called.

Instantly, the chimps stopped their temper tantrum and settled into silence. They each hung from the tree with one arm, watching Dr. Godfrey.

"How about some TV?" Dr. Godfrey asked. She sounded much calmer herself now. She picked up a remote control and aimed it at the television. At once, the chimps dropped to the ground and gathered in front of the TV as a program appeared on the screen. "Their favorite soap opera." Dr. Godfrey laughed. *"Days of Destiny."*

"Hi, Dr. Godfrey." A young man in a security

uniform entered the lab. He was in his early twenties, with reddish hair and wire-rimmed glasses. "Just came to visit my pals before my evening shift," he went on. "I see it's time for *Days of Destiny*."

"How are you, Tim?" Dr. Godfrey asked, moving to the desk.

For a moment, the Hardys watched the chimps watching the television set. The chimps weren't just viewing the soap opera—they were glued to it.

"I guess that's one more trait they share with humans," Joe joked. "Being couch potatoes!"

A minute later, the Hardys thanked Dr. Godfrey for her time and left the incredible world of Wendy, John, and Michael.

"What's your take on her?" Frank asked as the brothers strolled along a corridor.

"She's like somebody's mom," Joe said. "Nice and sweet, but if you mess with her kids—watch out. She seemed awfully angry about that funding cut. Maybe she wanted to create some bad publicity for the zoo in retaliation. I say she's definitely a suspect."

Frank agreed. "My thoughts exactly," he started. "In fact . . ." Suddenly he could feel a presence behind him. Somebody was listening! He spun around.

An enormous gorilla was pressed against the bars of his enclosure, staring at the Hardys. Frank knew

40

the ape could not get to him, but still he shivered. And after having seen how much language the chimps understood, he couldn't help but wonder if the gorilla had understood some of his conversation with Joe.

"Ready to exit Ape Avenue?" Joe asked.

"For sure," Frank said, checking his watch. "Actually, it's closing time. We'd better call it a day. I have a date tonight with Callie, and you've got one with Iola."

Joe winked at Frank and then yelled over to the gorilla, "Seen any good movies lately?"

By ten o'clock the next morning, the Hardys were back at the zoo and ready for action.

The first stop was the snow leopard enclosure, where they saw Chet sitting on a bench with Salamaji. Chet was being very attentive to the princess, who was wearing blue jeans and a T-shirt instead of a sari.

"Look at that." Joe laughed. "They're starting to look like a pair of lovebirds."

"Hi, Chet, Salamaji," Frank called out. When the princess looked up, Frank could see she had been crying.

"Uh-oh," Joe murmured. "Don't tell me Chet's broken her heart already."

"I don't know," Frank said as they drew closer. "Chet looks pretty upset, too. Something else must have happened."

Sure enough, Chet jumped to his feet a second later.

"I've got terrible news," he called out. "The snow leopard seems to have disappeared. And the zoo staff believes she was stolen!"

5 Endangered Species

"What do you mean, the snow leopard's missing?" Joe demanded.

"You see those rocks?" Chet pointed to the gunite rocks at the rear of the enclosure. "A door back there leads to a pen where the leopard spends the night. This morning when the keeper went to feed Emi, he found the pen empty. There's no way the animal could have escaped on her own, and she's nowhere in the area."

"Which means she must have been stolen," Frank concluded.

"We have to find Emi," Salamaji said, wiping a tear from her cheek. "We just have to!"

"We will," Chet promised, putting an arm around the princess. Then he turned back to the

Hardys. "I think Chase is in his office. He should have more details for you."

"Let's go," Joe said, already on the run.

Frank raced after his brother toward the administration building.

The zoo director was on the telephone in his office. He signaled for the Hardys to have a seat.

As he sat across a big mahogany desk from Chase, Joe glanced around at the dozens of animal photos on the wall, as well as a few African masks. Chase is really into animals, Joe thought. I guess it makes sense for a guy who is director of the zoo!

"Look," Chase was saying into the phone. "I don't have any more details for you now. I just don't—okay?" A second later, he hung up the receiver. "The press." He sighed with exasperation.

"We know about Emi," Frank jumped in. "What do you think happened?"

Before Chase could answer, the young security guard who'd visited the chimps yesterday walked into the room.

"Here's my report." The guard handed Chase a few papers. "I put in everything I could think of."

"Frank, Joe, meet Tim Peters, one of the night security guards," Chase said.

The guard waved. "Didn't I see you guys yesterday—at Dr. Godfrey's office?"

Frank nodded. "These boys are helping me investigate these unfortunate incidents," Chase explained.

Joe shot a glance at Frank. He'd been hoping Chase would keep their cover—especially since Dr. Godfrey thought they were "friends of the zoo."

"Nice to see you again," Peters said, covering a yawn. "Sorry, but I've been here about seventeen hours straight."

"Tim, could you tell the Hardys what you know about last night?" Chase requested.

"Sure," Peters said, removing his glasses to rub his eyes. "At one o'clock this morning, one of the guards heard an alarm go off at the aviary. Several of us raced over there and discovered someone had knocked a bunch of holes in the glass roof. Birds were escaping all over the place. We covered the holes right away and then all six guards on duty set about trying to retrieve the lost birds. We even stayed on after our shift was done at two. Fortunately, we got most of the birds back."

"What about the snow leopard?" Joe asked.

"When one of the cat keepers went to feed Emi this morning, he discovered she was gone," the guard explained. "Even though her pen was still locked."

"So she couldn't have broken out," Frank said.

"Is there an alarm there, too?" Joe asked.

"Yes." Peters nodded. "But I guess we were so busy going after those birds, we didn't hear it. And the alarm shuts off after about ten minutes."

"Also," Chase added, "we discovered a section

45

cut out of the fence that surrounds the zoo. That's probably how the thief got in and out."

"I feel awful about this, boss," Peters told Chase. "We should have been sharper."

The director shrugged. "It's a major loss for the zoo—not to mention bad publicity. But I don't hold any of the guards personally responsible. Obviously, this thing was very well planned."

"Good night, everybody," Peters said a few minutes later. "Uhm . . . I mean, good day."

"The police have been snooping around the zoo all morning," Chase remarked. "But so far they haven't come up with a thing. Whoever's behind these incidents is covering up his tracks pretty well."

"Last night's incident is different from the others," Frank pointed out. "An animal was stolen— not let loose. One crime is theft, the other is sabotage. The same party could be responsible for all the crimes, or we could be looking at two completely unrelated culprits."

"Good point," Joe said thoughtfully.

"Randy, got a sec?" came a voice.

Joe turned to see the eccentric millionaire, Theodore K. Anglethorpe, at the door. Today the hunter was wearing another safari shirt.

"Yeah, Ted." Chase waved him into the room. "Come on in."

"I stayed in town last night." Anglethorpe lowered his big body into a chair. "When I heard the news on the radio, I thought I'd stop by."

"Glad you did," Chase said. He then introduced the Hardys to Anglethorpe. Frank was glad Chase didn't mention the fact they were investigating the incidents at the zoo. The fewer people who knew, the better.

The conversation soon went back to the missing animal.

"The snow leopard is an endanged species, isn't it?" Joe asked.

"Correct," Chase said. "We estimate there are about four thousand of them left in the world."

"Technically, what does the term 'endangered species' mean?" Frank asked.

"About a quarter of the species on earth are becoming extinct," Anglethorpe spoke up. "Tigers, rhinos, gorillas, you name it. When the number of a certain species gets dangerously low, they're declared 'endangered.' That means it is against the law to kill them or profit from their parts in any way. Most of the countries of the world join together to enforce this law."

"One of the main goals of the modern zoo," Chase added, "is to breed these endangered species. Zoos do everything they can to keep them from dying out. That's why we were so excited about borrowing Ted's male snow leopard."

"Is it legal for a private citizen to own an endangered animal?" Frank asked Anglethorpe.

"If they have a special permit," Anglethorpe replied. "I purchased my snow leopard from a certified animal dealer, and I've got all the paperwork to prove it. But few people are granted this privilege."

"So it's hard for a private citizen to legally purchase an endangered animal," Frank said.

"Very," Chase confirmed.

Joe knew exactly where Frank was headed with his questions.

"Are there black markets for endangered animals?" he asked eagerly.

"Oh, yes." Anglethorpe nodded. "All sorts of them. Some endangered animals are sold as pets. Others are killed illegally so they can be made into fur coats. A snow leopard coat will run you about sixty thousand dollars these days. There's a black market for alligator skin as well. And, of course, one for rhino horns and one for the ivory that comes from the elephant tusks."

Chase shook his head. "They've even got ranches out in Texas where people pay large sums of money to hunt rare and endangered animals. Then the hunter gets the head as a trophy."

"It's astonishing," Anglethorpe added, "what some folks will do to make a buck."

"So it's possible," Frank began, looking back and forth between both men, "that Emi was stolen to be sold as a pet. Or for her fur. Or perhaps to be hunted."

"Even if the thief isn't planning to kill Emi," Chase said, "I still don't know if she'll survive."

Anglethorpe looked alarmed. "Why is that?"

"Her first few days at the zoo, she wouldn't eat,"

Chase revealed. "We discovered it was because she missed Salamaji so badly. Finally, we gave Emi a sari that belonged to the princess and that seemed to help the animal adjust. But without the scent of the princess nearby, I fear Emi may starve."

Joe was upset to hear this, too. With so few snow leopards left in the world, the Hardys had to find Emi.

"Okay, guys," Chase announced, "I've got a million phone calls to make. If you'll excuse me."

The meeting adjourned, the Hardys and Anglethorpe left the office together.

Joe found the wealthy hunter fascinating. He remembered Anglethorpe's saying he kept lots of animals on his island the other day at the press conference. Now he was dying to find out more. "How many animals do you own?" Joe asked him as they stepped outside into Zoo Plaza.

"Around thirty," Anglethorpe answered.

"I don't know too many people who have their own island," Frank put in. "Must be pretty amazing."

"It is." Anglethorpe chuckled. "My great-grandfather bought it. Very wealthy man. It's called Bitlow Island, and it's about, oh, forty miles out north on the bay. One of these days I'll be forced to get a real job, but for now I'm pretty happy out there. It's like my own private kingdom."

A few minutes later, Anglethorpe said goodbye and strolled away.

"Can you imagine having that many wild animals

right outside your door?" Joe said. "I'd love to see his island."

"Sorry, we weren't invited," Frank reminded his brother.

Just then Chet and Salamaji approached. The princess appeared calmer, but Frank could still see the sorrow in her brown eyes.

"Chet tells me if anyone can find Emi," Salamaji said, "it is the famous Hardy brothers. I hope he's right."

"We're doing our best," Joe told her.

"Any ideas?" Chet asked the brothers.

"Not yet," Joe admitted.

Frank glanced up to watch the monorail in the distance. Then he noticed something. Standing by the administration building was the boy who'd been watching the princess yesterday. Once more, the boy seemed to be staring at Salamaji.

"Salamaji," Frank said quietly. "There's a boy a short distance behind you. Take a quick look and see if you know him."

Salamaji knelt, as if to tie her shoe, and turned her head casually to see the boy. Then she let out a startled gasp.

"Who is it?" Joe asked.

"Please, let's go," Salamaji said, rising suddenly. "I want to get away from him." Salamaji began walking away from the plaza at a quick pace. Puzzled, Chet and the Hardys hurried after her.

"What's going on?" Chet asked.

"I'm not sure," Frank replied. Looking back, Frank noticed the teenage boy was following them.

The group walked quickly past a Native American totem pole, then came to a grassy enclosure where a herd of the legendary bison of the Old West were grazing. A bison lifted its massive shaggy head as the group passed by.

Glancing back, Frank saw the boy was still on their trail. "He's definitely pursuing us," he reported.

"Follow me," Chet said, taking the lead. Soon the group approached a black building with a replica of the moon on the roof. Chet ducked inside. "We can lose him in here," he called.

As soon as Frank, Joe, Chet, and the princess entered the building, they were plunged into a world of almost complete darkness. A few tiny red lights were blinking to help them adjust their eyes.

"This is the Night World exhibit," Chet whispered. "They keep nocturnal creatures in here. The ones that sleep by day and come awake at night."

"Cool," Joe said, heading for a sign that explained some facts about nocturnal animals. "Check this out."

"Ouch!" Frank exclaimed suddenly. "You stepped on my foot."

"Sorry," Joe apologized. "I guess my eyes still aren't used to the dark!"

A few minutes later, the group moved along a winding corridor. Though other visitors were present, everyone seemed to be keeping their voices very low, as if afraid of awakening dangerous creatures. From time to time, Frank stole backward glances, making sure the mysterious boy hadn't entered Night World. He wanted to ask Salamaji more about who the boy was, but his instincts told him this wasn't the time. The princess hadn't said a word—clearly she wasn't ready to explain the boy's identity.

"Take a look." Chet pointed to a large rectangular window. Behind the glass, in eerie dim light, was a simulated jungle setting. A miniature version of an alligator lingered by a small pond. Above, little furry shapes clung upside down to a series of ropelike tree branches.

"What are those?" Salamaji asked. "Rats?"

"No, bats!" Chet replied.

As if on cue, the bats suddenly came to life. In perfect unison, they dropped from the branches, extended their long rubbery wings, and began soaring madly about the display case.

"Ooooh." Salamaji shuddered. "They are so frightening."

Frank glanced back one more time but still saw no sign of the mysterious boy. I guess we lost him, he thought.

"I see why Salamaji thought they were rats," Joe said. "These guys look a lot like rodents."

Chet nodded. "Bats are really interesting animals," he said.

"They can't see very well, but they have a

highly sophisticated sonar system in their ears, which helps them find their way around. Come on, I have to show you something else."

Chet led the group through a crowd of people to another window. Inside, more bats were flapping wildly behind the glass. "Wait till you see these," Chet said.

"Wow," Joe declared. "Vampire bats."

Frank had heard about vampire bats, but he'd never gotten a chance to see one for himself till today. He watched the creatures soar through the darkness.

"Why are they called vampire bats?" Joe asked.

"They attach themselves to sleeping mammals and slowly, drop by drop, suck out their blood," Chet said in a dramatic tone. "Am I scaring you, Salamaji? Salamaji?"

But Salamaji did not answer.

"Salamaji!" Chet said louder.

Frank looked about, his heart racing. For a second, he refused to believe what his eyes were telling him: Salamaji was gone.

How could he have let her out of his sight—for even a second?

A terrifying sound interrupted Frank's thoughts. From off in the distance came a female scream!

6 The Most Dangerous Creature

For the next second, Night World was completely silent.

Then a nervous buzz filled the air. All the visitors were wondering who had screamed and why.

Frantically, Frank tried to pinpoint the direction of the scream. Joe gripped his arm.

"I'm pretty sure that was Salamaji," Joe murmured. "We've got to find her."

"And her mysterious friend," Frank added grimly.

Chet was scanning Night World desperately.

"Salamaji!" he called. "Salamaji!"

"She can't have gone far," Frank told him. "We'll find her. Let's split up and search this place."

Frank, Joe, and Chet took off in separate directions through the dark corridors of Night World.

Every few minutes, one of them yelled out the princess's name, but there was no answer.

Suddenly Frank saw someone standing in the shadows of a distant corner.

"Salamaji?" Frank asked as he approached. "Salamaji, is that you?"

"No, it's not," came a gruff voice. In the dim light, Frank made out an older man talking on a cellular phone.

"Sorry," Frank mumbled. He continued down the corridor, past several display cases, then stepped through an exit door. Immediately, he was blinded by the daylight. After blinking a few times to adjust his eyes, Frank saw Salamaji standing beneath a tree in the distance. She was with the mysterious boy who had been following her, and they seemed to be arguing.

Frank raced over. Instantly, Salamaji and the boy stopped their discussion. The boy looked away, as if he was trying to control intense anger.

"Are you all right?" Frank asked the princess. "We heard a scream, and . . ."

"I'm fine," Salamaji said, nervously fingering her long black hair. But Frank sensed she wasn't telling the truth.

Joe and Chet ran up to join the group before Frank could ask more questions.

"What's going on?" Chet demanded. "Who is this guy? What happened in there?"

The boy glared at Chet with dark brown eyes. Then he spoke to Salamaji in an accent similar to hers. "I will leave you with your new friends for now. However, Your Highness, I am not finished with you. No, I am definitely not finished."

The boy stalked away without looking back.

"Who is he, Salamaji?" Joe asked.

"He is a boy from my country," Salamaji explained curtly. "He also goes to Bayport University."

Chet looked confused. "What did he want?"

"Nothing special." Salamaji jammed her hands in her jeans pockets and looked away as she spoke. "He came up behind me in the Night World. That's why I screamed. Then he pulled me outside. I am sorry if I scared anyone."

Frank eyed the princess suspiciously. "If he didn't want anything special, why were you so anxious to get away from him?"

Salamaji met his gaze evenly. "Now I see I was just acting silly. It is . . . what's the phrase? No big deal."

Reluctantly, Frank dropped the issue. It was obvious there was more to the story, but there wasn't much he could do if Salamaji wasn't talking.

"Okay, let's get back to work," Frank told Joe. "First, I'd like to pay those animal activists the Kellermans a visit. Their office address is on that pamphlet they gave us yesterday."

"Good idea," Joe agreed. Before saying goodbye to Salamaji and Chet, Frank pulled his friend aside. "See if you can get Salamaji to give you some more info on that guy who was following her," he said. "I want to know what he's up to. It could be important to the case."

"I'll do what I can," Chet told him.

Glancing up, Joe noticed more gray clouds gliding ominously across the sky. "It's definitely going to rain," he predicted. "Let's get going before we get soaked."

An hour later the Hardys parked their van on a side street of downtown Bayport.

"We're in the low-rent district," Joe reminded Frank as he took in the run-down buildings and litter-strewn street. "I guess the Kellermans aren't too well funded."

Frank nodded. "We'll play this one by ear," he said. "I'll come up with a cover for our visit."

The Hardys walked to a grimy gray building on the corner and went inside. They climbed four steep flights of steps, then came to a door marked 403. Rock music blared loudly from a radio inside.

Joe knocked hard, and a moment later Janet Kellerman opened the door.

"Oh, it's you," she said, looking unpleasantly surprised. "What do you want?"

"We read your pamphlet." Frank had to shout over the music. "We're . . . uh, interested in doing some volunteer work for your organization."

Janet hesitated, then said, "Come in."

The Hardys stepped into the ARF headquarters, which consisted of a single room. There were two desks, a filing cabinet, and messy piles of paper all over the place.

Jeff Kellerman was sitting at a desk. He waved at the Hardys.

"Before we commit to anything," Joe said over the music, "could you give us a little more information about Animal Rights Force?"

Janet snapped off the radio.

"Sit down," Jeff said, indicating two metal chairs.

Frank and Joe sat in the chairs. Immediately, Jeff swung his chair around and glared at them. Janet remained standing, hovering over them nervously. Suddenly, Joe felt as if he were on trial.

"Do you know what the most dangerous creature in the world is?" Jeff demanded.

"The elephant?" Joe guessed.

"Wrong," Jeff Kellerman shot back.

"I think he means us," Frank told Joe.

"That's right." Jeff nodded vigorously. "Human beings. Homo sapiens. We are the most dangerous creatures of all."

"One-fourth of all the species on earth are disappearing," Janet put in. "And why is that? Because all over the globe, man is destroying the world these animals live in. In our infinite greed, we snatch more wood, more oil, more crops from the earth. And if we're not destroying the habitats of these animals, we kill them for their hides or fur or bones or tusks."

"Not only are we destroying certain species," Jeff picked up, "but we are making life painful and

58

miserable for many other animals as well. Some animals are used for research in laboratories. Others are forced to perform in circuses and carnivals."

"And let's not forget zoos," Janet added.

"But wait," Frank interrupted. "Zoos treat their animals very well. They feed them, take care of their illnesses, and for the most part give them plenty of space. Most of the animals at the Bayport Zoo look pretty content to me."

"And zoos are the last hope for a lot of species," Joe put in. "The zoos are doing everything they can to breed endangered animals and keep them from becoming extinct."

"Animals don't belong in captivity," Janet snapped. She slammed her hand down on a nearby desk. "They should be left in the wild in peace. That is their natural right!"

"There are the artificial laws made by man," Jeff said, leaning toward the Hardys. "And then there is a higher law. The law of Nature."

Frank considered this for a moment before speaking. "Do you ever break the laws of man to serve the laws of Nature?" he asked finally.

Jeff and Janet looked at each other.

"No," Janet answered. "My husband and I never break the government's laws—even if we don't believe in them."

"If we go around breaking laws, we'll end up in jail," Jeff added, picking up an envelope. "And then we won't be of any use at all. Will we?"

Frank was watching the Kellermans carefully. "So what is it you two do exactly?" he asked.

"We do a lot of protesting," Janet said, folding her arms across her chest. "And we spend a lot of time writing letters and making phone calls. In general, our mission is to draw attention to our cause. Any way we can."

"I see," Frank said thoughtfully. "And would you have any use for us as volunteers?"

"I'll tell you what," Jeff said, handing Frank two books. "I'm going to lend you some books about animal abuse. After you've read them, if you're still interested, give us a call."

Before Joe could say something, Janet interrupted. "We'd better get moving, Jeff." She went over to the closet and opened the door. Joe turned back to Jeff as she reached inside.

Abruptly, Jeff stood. "My wife and I have an appointment. Come on, we'll walk you out."

After locking up their office, the Kellermans walked the Hardys down to the street. Jeff and Janet said goodbye, then hurried over to a beat-up green Chevrolet parked down the block.

"Should we trail them?" Joe asked as both brothers climbed inside the van.

"Not now," Frank replied. "But at least we've seen their car. That may come in handy."

"I'm not sure I bought that stuff about never breaking the law," Joe said. "How about we take a look around their office? Unchaperoned this time."

"Exactly what I was thinking," Frank said, watching the Chevrolet drive away.

Joe grabbed some equipment from the back of the van, and the Hardys hurried back up to Room 403. Joe quickly inserted a long metal device in the cylinder of the Kellermans' office door and slid the lock open. The Hardys stepped into the office and went to work. While Joe searched the filing cabinet, Frank studied the phone machine. He quickly figured out the machine's entry code, in case they needed to tap into the Kellermans' messages. Next, he leafed through papers on the desk. The only interesting thing he found was a memo: "See Bill at Specialty Express, 10 A.M., Aug. 7." He quickly jotted down the information.

Joe pulled out a file of newspaper clippings and scanned them. All of the articles pertained to some form of animal abuse: lab research, zoos, hunting, poaching, and so forth. Nothing caught Joe's interest until he spotted a headline: "Couple Suspected of Freeing Lab Animals." Joe read the article, then let out a low whistle. "Listen to this, Frank. A year ago in St. Louis, Missouri, a bunch of test animals—chimpanzees, rats, snakes—were stolen from a lab where medical research was being conducted. No one was arrested, but apparently Jeff and Janet Kellerman were suspected of the crime. The lab didn't prosecute because it was afraid of the bad publicity."

"Hmmm." Frank moved in to look at the clip-

61

ping. "But the Kellermans were never proven guilty of the crime."

"Still, it makes you wonder," Joe commented. "You know, maybe—"

"Joe, don't move," Frank whispered.

"Why not?" Joe said, looking up from the file.

Then Joe got his answer. Coiled on top of the filing cabinet, mere inches from Joe's wrist, was a three-foot-long snake. The snake's skin was blue and green with black stripes.

Joe gulped. "Is this the Kellermans' security system?"

"It might be," Frank went on slowly. "And I'm betting it's a *poisonous* security system."

Beads of sweat trickled down Joe's forehead. He was well aware of how fast snakes could strike. He stayed very still as he said, "Maybe that's why Janet opened the closet door before she left. To let Slimey here out for his watch."

Frank nodded. "Don't move—whatever you do."

Every impulse was telling Joe to run like crazy, but he stood still while Frank gazed around the room. Joe's eyes were locked on the snake dangling over him.

Suddenly, the snake's head shot forward, aiming for Joe's wrist.

Joe felt the dry scaly snakeskin slither against his own skin as the creature began wrapping itself around his forearm!

7 Night Quarters

Frank stared in horror at the snake coiled around his brother's arm. He tried to stay calm and act as if he knew exactly what he was doing.

"I'm going to find something to pry it off with," he said in an even tone. "Keep still."

"Easy for you to say," Joe remarked as the snake slid its way upward by making continual loops around his arm.

Stay cool, Joe thought, forcing himself to concentrate on the snake's skin. He noticed it was composed of tiny interlocking scales and bright blue and green colors. He shuddered as the snake shot out a long tongue for a split-second.

"Hurry, Frank," Joe whispered.

"Coming." Frank returned with a wire hanger that he had straightened out. Very slowly, Frank eased the end of the hanger toward the snake's boneless body. The snake stopped and looked at Frank.

"Don't get him mad," Joe whispered.

"No problem," Frank returned. "I've got the situation under control."

Joe made himself take a deep breath as the snake continued up his arm. He could almost see the snake's mouth opening, almost feel the deadly fangs sinking into his neck. . . .

With a single deft move, Frank slipped the hanger under the creature's belly and yanked the snake off Joe's arm. He flipped the reptile straight up into the air.

"Run!" Frank ordered.

Joe didn't need to be told twice. The brothers barreled out of the room and Frank slammed the door behind them.

Joe's face was pale and his whole body was trembling as they stood outside Room 403.

"I thought the Kellermans were against keeping animals in captivity," he said weakly.

Frank nodded. "I have a feeling those two break lots of laws," he said. "The kind made by man *and* the kind made by Nature."

"Let's get out of here," Joe said. As the Hardys took off down the stairs, he glanced nervously behind him to check the crack under the door. It looked just wide enough for a snake to slither through.

A few minutes later, Frank was driving the van

toward a fast-food place for lunch, while Joe talked on a cellular telephone. He was checking out the clue in the memo Frank had found on the Kellermans' desk.

"Listen to this," he said, setting the phone down a moment later. "Specialty Express is a small cargo airline that operates out of the Bayport Airport. It specializes in shipping oddball items. Especially live animals and things that need refrigeration."

Frank shot a glance at Joe. "Very interesting," he said, shifting his eyes back to the traffic ahead.

Frank switched lanes, then turned into the entrance of the Yummy Burger restaurant. They ordered some burgers and fries at a takeout window, then took off.

"Okay," Frank said as he bit into a burger, "the Kellermans said they like to draw attention to their cause. Any way they can. They deny that includes breaking the law, but we have our doubts."

"So maybe they staged those animal escapes to make the zoo look bad," Joe said, handing Frank a soft drink. "But why would they single out the snow leopard to steal?"

"Emi's appearance got a lot of press coverage," Frank said. "And her disappearance will probably get even more. Mr. Anglethorpe said he already heard about it on the radio. And the fact that the snow leopard is a member of an endangered species makes the zoo look even worse. I'd say we've got a pretty strong motive for the Kellermans."

"So maybe they kidnapped Emi," Joe speculated as he unwrapped his hamburger, "and they're planning to ship her somewhere via Specialty Express."

"They have an appointment there at ten tomorrow morning," Frank replied. "If we haven't found Emi by then, let's stake out the airport. In the meantime, I want to keep a close watch on the zoo tonight."

"I like the way you think, brother," Joe said. Then he concentrated on polishing off his food.

The Hardys entered the zoo just as the grounds were closing for the night. Though it still had not rained, the gray clouds were stubbornly refusing to leave the sky. The brothers made a beeline for the administration building.

Randy Chase was in his office, going through some paperwork. "The Bayport police still have no leads," Chase told them. "And your friend, Chet, wanted me to report he wasn't able to get any more information on that guy following Salamaji." He looked at Frank and Joe hopefully. "Please tell me the brilliant Hardy brothers have solved everything by now."

"Afraid not." Frank shook his head. "But since the sabotages were carried out at night, we'd like to observe the zoo grounds tonight. Maybe we'll get some ideas or clues that way."

"This will also give us a chance to meet the night security staff," Joe added. "I think they should all be investigated."

Chase nodded, then picked up his walkie-talkie and spoke into it. "Peters, it's Randy Chase. Would you stop by my office, please?"

Five minutes later Tim Peters entered the office, wearing his security uniform and looking considerably more awake than he had that morning. "Tim," the zoo director said, "Frank and Joe would like to spend some time on the grounds tonight. Would you mind showing them around some?"

"I'd be glad to," Peters said, flashing a friendly smile. "Follow me, guys."

Peters led the Hardys to a zoo Jeep parked outside.

"There are two nighttime security shifts," Peters explained as he put the vehicle in gear. "The first runs from six to two; the other runs from two to ten. There are six guards for each shift."

"Wow." Joe shook his head. "I can't imagine working all night like that."

"It gets pretty rough sometimes," Peters admitted.

He turned into the entrance of the cat compound and parked the Jeep by a fenced-off area. With a key from the big ring on his belt, he unlocked the fence, then led the Hardys to a small building.

"This area is for zoo staff only," Peters warned. "It can be dangerous around here so—"

Suddenly, a vicious roar echoed through the building. Joe jumped, making Peters grin.

"That's one of the tigers," the guard explained, pointing to a barred door in the building. "He just had some raw meat for dinner and was hoping you might be dessert."

"My brother tastes better," Joe told the tiger.

Through the bars, Frank saw the orange Bengal tiger who had escaped the day before. "Remember, you guys don't like to eat people," Frank said to the cat as it licked its paw with a long pink tongue.

The Hardys followed Peters to another small building. He unlocked the barred door and led them into a small room with concrete walls and a tiled floor.

"This is the snow leopard's night quarters," Peters explained.

"Why are the animals put in night quarters?" Joe asked, glancing at the empty room. "Why can't they sleep in their daytime habitats?"

"So they can't hurt anybody if some loony breaks in at night," Peters said. "Also so they can't get stolen. Except this is the room Emi *was* stolen from."

Peters led the Hardys through a door into a narrow chamber with a hose, shovel, and other maintenance supplies. Peters pulled up on a lever. A steel door in the wall mechanically opened. "This way." Peters gestured.

Stooping over, the Hardys stepped through the low door and found themselves standing on Emi's Himalayan mountainside.

"In the morning, Emi would go through this door to get outside," Peters explained. "Then she'd come back through at night. The animals are only fed in the buildings, once in the morning and then again in the evening."

"The culprit would have to get through several locks to get to Emi," Joe commented.

"Locks can be picked," Peters said with a shrug. "Or else it was someone who had keys."

Joe glanced at the ring of keys on Peters's belt.

For another hour or so, the Hardys followed Peters on his rounds, which consisted mostly of driving around, making sure nothing was amiss. The Hardys also got Peters to introduce them to the rest of the first-shift night security team. The five other guards ranged in age from twenty-five to about seventy. Joe was hoping the Hardys would get to question some of them later in more detail.

By eight-thirty darkness had settled over the grounds, and Peters drove back to Zoo Plaza.

"I have some paperwork to do inside," he said. "Anything else I can show you?"

"Could we wander around a bit?" Joe asked.

"I suppose so," Peters said, adjusting his glasses. "Everything wild is locked safely away. I'll be around until two A.M., if you need me."

"Thanks," Joe said, jumping out of the Jeep. Frank and Joe walked across the dark empty zoo grounds. They weren't quite sure what they were looking for, mostly anything suspicious. Crickets chirped, but otherwise it was quiet.

"It's creepy in here at night," Joe said, passing

69

the empty hippopotamus swamp. "You can't see anything, but it's like there are a thousand hidden eyes watching you."

Suddenly, a weird cooing sound pierced the darkness.

Frank snapped his head around. "What was that?"

"Your guess is as good as mine," Joe replied.

"Let's head over to the reptile house," Frank suggested. "I want to get a better look at that python's escape route."

At the reptile house, Frank looked up at the exterior vent through which the python had escaped.

"You know something," he said thoughtfully, "all of the sabotages involved getting to a high place. This vent, the hot wire in the macaque exhibit, and the tree limb in the tiger habitat."

Joe nodded. "The hot-wire in the macaque enclosure looks especially tough to reach," he agreed.

"A security guard would have access to a ladder," Frank reasoned. "And I guess the Kellermans might be in good enough shape to climb pretty well." He paused, thinking about their other suspect. "What about Dr. Godfrey? She's not all that young. Could she get to those places by herself?"

"She could have gotten someone to help her," Joe suggested. "You know, an accomplice."

Frank thought about this as he stared up at the vent. Dr. Godfrey probably had several assistants, and they might also be upset about the funding cuts. Maybe she recruited . . . Frank's eyes lit up like light bulbs switching on.

"Pop quiz," he said suddenly. "Can you name three of Dr. Godfrey's friends who are especially good at climbing? Hint, they may not be human."

"Wendy, John, and Michael!" Joe exclaimed.

"Right!" Frank whirled toward his brother. "Dr. Godfrey said they could learn practically anything, and, remember, they had hammers and other tools in their toy chest. Maybe Godfrey trained the chimps to use the necessary tools. Then she could have taken them to the sabotage sites at night when no guards were around. The chimps could easily climb to those hard-to-reach spots—and, presto, they do the job."

"It's crazy," Joe said, eyeing the drainpipe on the side of the building. "But it also makes perfect sense. Come on, let's go test our theory."

The Hardys hurried to the ape building and found one of the exterior doors unlocked.

"Quiet," Joe whispered, "there may be a guard somewhere in the building."

The Hardys crept past the sleeping gorillas and soon came to the chimpanzee laboratory. Joe was prepared to pick the lock when he noticed this door was also unlocked.

"That's funny," he began.

"Maybe the guard's in here," Frank whispered.

The Hardys entered the lab, finding the room

71

dimly lit by a desk lamp. Joe didn't see any humans in the room, and peering beyond the bars, he didn't see the chimps either.

"Where are they?" Joe wondered out loud.

"In the tree," Frank whispered.

Then Joe saw Wendy, John, and Michael stretched out on tree limbs, sound asleep. Suddenly, Wendy opened her eyes and peered at the Hardys. She rustled a branch and her two brothers also awakened. One by one, the chimps dropped noiselessly to the floor.

"Shhh," Frank urged, a finger to his lips. The chimps each put a finger to their lips as if they understood. "Tools," he whispered, pointing to the toy chest. "Can you get the tools?"

Wendy scampered on all fours to the toy chest and began pulling out various tools. John and Michael watched curiously, and Joe quickly realized that Wendy was the group's leader. Soon Wendy had laid out on the floor a hammer, saw, wrench, pliers, ruler, scissors, and several screwdrivers.

"Scissors to clip the hot-wire," Joe observed. "A screwdriver to unscrew the vent. And a saw to sever the tree limb. Everything they need is right there. Now, let's see if they can use all the tools."

"Saw," Frank whispered to the chimps, making a sawing gesture. "Can you saw wood?"

Wendy nodded, then found a piece of wood, which she handed to John and Michael. She picked up the small saw, and as the brother chimps held the wood, Wendy began sawing through it with the skill of an experienced carpenter.

"Son of a gun," Joe whispered in disbelief. "They can do it. Those chimps could have actually done the sabotage!"

Suddenly, the cage door clicked. Frank turned, wondering if someone had released the electronic lock in the adjoining office.

Before Frank and Joe could secure the door, Wendy sprang into action. She swung open the door and all three chimps bounded into the room, screeching noisily in delight. They were free!

Joe looked at Frank. "Somebody must have seen us come in here," he remarked. "I bet somebody wanted to put a stop to our experiment."

"You may be right," Frank agreed. "The question is, are they going to be joining us?"

Joe looked at the chimps, who were running and jumping all over the room. "We'd better get these guys back in their room before we do any investigating."

John scampered up to Joe. The chimp grabbed Joe's right hand and began shaking it vigorously.

"Nice to meet you, too," Joe said, uncertain whether the chimp was being friendly or hostile.

Wendy jumped on Frank's back. "Hey, get down!" Frank cried. Instead, Wendy reached her head around and gave Frank a kiss on the cheek. In spite of the situation, Frank laughed. "Wait till Callie hears a *chimp* kissed me!"

A second later the chimps' playful mood seemed

to change. As little Michael began jumping on the desktop, John pulled Joe's arm behind his back and twisted it upward.

"Hey!" Joe yelled. "That hurts!"

The chimps kept screeching, sounding louder and wilder.

Then Wendy wrapped an arm around Frank's neck and began applying pressure.

"No," Frank scolded, trying to pull the arm away. But Wendy's slender hairy arm was incredibly strong, and Frank couldn't budge it. "Stop it!" Frank choked out the words. "Stop it!"

But Wendy's grip kept tightening, and Frank realized the chimp was strangling him!

8 A Trail of Blood

"Accch!" Frank gasped, struggling to breathe.

"Owwww!" Joe yelled as the chimp twisted his arm behind his back. "He's going to break my arm!"

Joe couldn't believe the animals' strength—so this was why Dr. Godfrey had warned them about the chimps! If he and Frank didn't figure a way out soon, these chimps could do some real damage.

Meanwhile, the littlest chimp, Michael, began picking papers off the desk and tossing them wildly into the air. All three chimps were screeching with glee, apparently having more fun than a barrelful of monkeys.

"Idea . . ." Frank was trying to tell Joe something. "Zoo friends . . ."

Instantly, Joe got it. He needed to remind the chimps that he and Frank were too important to hurt.

"Zoo friends!" Joe shouted. "Remember, we're zoo friends! Zoo friends! We give money!"

The chimps didn't seem to care. Joe watched helplessly as Wendy's grip on Frank tightened. His brother's face drained of color.

"Sign . . ." Frank struggled to speak, but Wendy's viselike arm cut off his words. Frank waved a hand frantically, hoping Joe would understand.

"Right," Joe called back. Pain shot through his arm as John held it pinned against Joe's back. With his free hand, Joe waved at Wendy until he got her attention. Then he slowly made the hand signs for "zoo friends." Luckily he had watched Dr. Godfrey closely yesterday.

From her perch on Frank's back, Wendy kept her eyes fixed on Joe. Desperately he made the hand signs again while speaking very clearly. "Zoo friends, zoo friends, zoo friends!" he said over and over.

Finally, Wendy's screeching subsided. Frank felt the pressure on his neck ease. As Frank gulped in a big breath of air, Wendy dropped off his back and scampered over to John. She pulled her brother away from Joe, making the hand signs for "zoo friends."

"Talk about your close call," Joe murmured. He massaged his aching right arm.

76

"I'll say," Frank agreed. He glanced at the adjoining office. "Why don't you find out if we're alone in here, and I'll try to handle our ape friends."

Little Michael was still dancing on the desktop, screeching "eeeh-eeeh-eeeh" and throwing papers into the air. But then, seeing the party was over, he stopped and started scratching his chin in confusion.

Joe rushed into the adjoining office while Frank tried to think of a way to get the chimps back into the caged area.

"Money!" Frank called, suddenly pulling a few dollar bills from his wallet. Talking about "zoo friends" had worked a moment ago—maybe reminding them that "zoo friends" gave money would do the trick now. . . .

Frank placed three bills inside the barred area.

One by one, the three chimps scampered over to get the bills, snatching them up and examining them closely. With a sigh of relief, Frank shut the barred door after them, hearing the door automatically lock.

"Nothing like a little bribery," he muttered.

"No sign of anyone around," Joe reported as he came running in through the hallway door. "There's another door from the office to the hallway so someone could have easily come and gone without our seeing them."

Frank nodded, then stooped down to pick up the

papers Michael had scattered everywhere. "Maybe Dr. Sara Godfrey was in her office when we got here," he remarked. "Remember, the lab door was open. Maybe she didn't want us to see just how good those chimpanzees are with those tools."

"Those chimps definitely could have assisted with the sabotage," Joe said, rubbing his sore arm. "In fact, they seem specially trained for the job."

"And we know Godfrey has a big grudge against the zoo." Frank placed papers on the desk. "So she's got a motive."

Looking over at the chimps, Frank was surprised to see they were now chewing on his dollar bills.

Joe followed his brother's gaze. "I guess you're out a few bucks," he commented.

"Seemed cheaper to bribe them than pay with my life!" Frank retorted.

A few minutes later, the Hardys left the ape building and walked across the deserted zoo grounds. A slight breeze rustled the trees, followed by a low rumble of thunder.

"Let's get a bite to eat," Joe suggested. "Being attacked by chimps always make me hungry."

"Okay," Frank agreed quickly. "I've had enough of the zoo for tonight anyway. We can check out the airport first thing in the morning and see what the Kellermans are up to."

As the Hardys hurried toward the parking lot, a mysterious howl cut through the night.

"You know . . ." Joe took a last look around the

dark zoo. "This zoo is turning into a very wild place."

Shortly before nine A.M., Frank and Joe were seated at a far end of the Bayport Airport terminal building, waiting for the Kellermans to arrive. Their faces were hidden by the morning edition of the *Bayport Gazette* bearing the headline "Snow Leopard Stolen from the Bayport Zoo."

"I've been thinking," Joe said, keeping his head below the newspaper. "We haven't had a chance to talk to many of the security guards, except Tim. He seems friendly, but . . ."

"But what?" Frank asked.

"Doesn't it seem odd that he knows so much about the chimps?" Joe asked. "Remember how he came by to visit them the other day? He also knew what their favorite soap opera was. Maybe, for some reason, he's in on the sabotage with Godfrey. It's a long shot, but I say we check him out a little more carefully."

"Heads up. Jeff and Janet," Frank whispered.

Peering discreetly around his paper, Joe saw the Kellermans enter the building and make their way to the counter marked Specialty Express. Janet began speaking with a young man at the counter. Soon the man showed Janet a sheet of paper, and Jeff moved closer and seemed to be making some notes.

"What's he writing?" Joe asked quietly.

79

"Got me," Frank said.

Next, the young man extended his arms far apart.

"It looks like he's demonstrating the size of a container or crate," Frank said, watching carefully. "Could it be large enough for Emi?"

"Pretty close," Joe answered.

A minute later, the Kellermans left the counter and headed out of the terminal building.

"Let's follow them," Frank said.

Joe was already on his feet. Outside in the parking lot, the Hardys trailed the couple to their green Chevrolet. Suddenly thunder boomed overhead.

"I think that storm's about to break," Joe said, noticing black clouds gathering in the sky like an army preparing for battle.

As the Kellermans drove out of the parking lot, the Hardys hopped into their van.

"Let's rock 'n' roll," Frank said, his foot on the accelerator. Then, using his expert tracking skills, Frank began trailing the Chevrolet on a serpentine path through the city.

"Maybe the Kellermans really did kidnap Emi," Frank said, eyes on the road. "And now they're planning to send her somewhere. Maybe back to the Himalayas."

"But that kills our theory about the chimps," Joe answered.

"Not necessarily." Frank turned on his headlights as the sky darkened. "Don't forget, the sabotage and theft of Emi could be two completely separate crimes."

"Right," Joe said. The Chevrolet led the Hardys to a quiet street lined with large windowless buildings. There wasn't a soul outside.

"These are mostly warehouses," Joe said, watching the Chevrolet slow down.

The Kellermans parked at the far end of the empty street, and Frank stopped at the near corner. Jeff and Janet climbed out of their car and walked toward one of the warehouses, each of them carrying a plastic bag.

"What are they up to?" Frank murmured.

The Kellermans stopped at the door of one of the warehouses, looking around furtively.

Frank and Joe watched from the van as Jeff rigged a small boxlike device onto the door.

"What the—?" Joe whispered.

KAPOW! A small explosion at the door cut off his words.

"A bomb!" Frank exclaimed. "These guys aren't just activists; they're terrorists!" In a flash the Hardys jumped out of the van. Outside, on the street, an alarm began wailing. The Kellermans slipped inside the warehouse.

Joe took off. "Wait here, Frank," he yelled over his shoulder. "Watch the door!"

Frank jumped back into the van. All of a sudden, the rain began pouring so furiously that Frank could see nothing but sheets of water through the windshield. As the rain slapped noisily against the van, Frank flipped on the wipers.

Frank waited. And waited. He watched the rain slash violently against the buildings and pavement and windshield. Then he watched the wipers swish endlessly back and forth, back and forth, and soon Frank found himself impatiently tapping out the wipers' rhythm on the steering wheel.

Ten minutes went by, but it seemed like an eternity to Frank. What's going on inside, he wondered. It would be two against one in there. And what else did the Kellermans have in those bags?

As a jagged bolt of lightning streaked the sky, Frank finally saw Jeff and Janet step out of the warehouse. They stood by the door a moment, an overhead ledge protecting them from the downpour. Janet was holding both bags and Jeff was wiping his hands with a handkerchief.

Peering as hard as he could through the slashing rain, Frank realized Jeff Kellerman's handkerchief was stained bright red. It seemed the man was wiping blood from his hands!

There was another burst of thunder, and the Kellermans made a dash for their car. With a pounding heart, Frank watched the Kellermans climb into their car and drive off into the ferocious storm.

Frank swung out of the van, flew to the warehouse, and barreled through the door. "Joe!" Frank called, finding himself inside a giant darkened space. "Where are you!"

There was no answer. Frank felt along a wall and managed to turn on an overhead fluorescent light.

The warehouse was filled with racks of fur coats—mink, fox, sable, and chinchilla. Then Frank noticed blood dripping from some of the coats.

"Joe!" Frank called loudly. Still no answer.

Then Frank's heart stopped. A trail of fresh blood was splattered across the floor!

9 The Missing Princess

Frank followed the splotches of blood down an aisle of coats until the trail led him to the back of the warehouse. There Frank found an overturned rack of furs sprawled on the floor.

Suddenly, one of the furs moved.

"Joe?" Frank called cautiously. Hearing a muffled response, Frank threw several coats out of the way and found his brother lying on the ground.

"Oh, no!" Frank cried in horror. Joe's face and shirt were covered with blood!

"I'm okay." Joe groaned, slowly lifting his head. "Really, I am."

"You're soaked in blood!" Frank exclaimed.

"It's not blood," Joe said, wiping red from his face. "It's red paint. Latex, fortunately."

"Wh-wh . . ." Frank stammered.

"This is a fur-coat warehouse," Joe said groggily. "The Kellermans, of course, are against animals being killed for furs, so they came here to make a point." Joe gestured toward a wall, and Frank turned to look.

Emblazoned on the wall, in dripping red paint, were the words "All of these animals were murdered!"

"They brought cans of red paint with them," Joe said, sitting up. "Janet painted the message while Jeff went around tossing paint on coats. I watched them a few minutes behind a rack, but then I tripped on something and they came after me. I turned my head so they wouldn't see me, and Jeff threw paint at my face so I wouldn't see him. Then he shoved a rack at me and I guess it knocked me out for a minute."

Frank shook his head. "Now we know that the Kellermans really do break the laws of man to serve the laws of Nature."

Joe nodded, his eyes on the dripping message. "Come on. Let's go home so I can change into something less . . . bloody."

The rain had let up as Frank drove the blue van homeward.

"Okay, review time," Joe said, watching the steady swish of the windshield wipers. "It's day three on the case, and so far we have three prime suspect groups. The Kellermans; Dr. Godfrey and the chimps; and the boy from Rashipah."

"We have good motives for two of these groups,"

Frank remarked, "and plenty of suspicious action from all of them. The problem is, we don't have any conclusive proof on any of them."

"Right," Joe said. "Plus we have to check into Peters today."

Frank steered the van into the driveway of the Hardys' home at 23 Elm Street. The Hardys jumped out and dashed through the rain to the back porch.

"Aunt Gertrude is probably watching TV in the living room," Frank cautioned. "We'll sneak into the kitchen so she doesn't see that paint and pass out."

"Good point." Joe gave his brother a thumbs-up. The last thing he wanted was to scare Aunt Gertrude, who lived with the Hardys and tended to fuss over her detective nephews.

Joe opened the back door and stepped inside. Instantly, he heard a bloodcurdling scream!

"Wait!" Joe cried. "I'm all right!"

Aunt Gertrude was standing in the kitchen, dramatically clutching her heart.

"Joseph!" Aunt Gertrude shrieked. "You are certainly *not* all right!"

"It's red paint," Joe assured her. "I just had a little, uh, accident."

"Oh my, oh my, oh my." Aunt Gertrude sighed, leaning on a counter. "I was watching a soap opera, and during the commercial, I came in here to get a soda, and there you are looking like—something from a horror movie!"

"What soap were you watching?" Frank asked suddenly.

"*Days of Destiny,*" Aunt Gertrude confessed. "My favorite. Why do you ask?"

Frank and Joe looked at each other, then grinned. That was also the chimps' favorite soap opera.

"What's so funny?" Aunt Gertrude demanded.

Before Frank could answer, the front door flew open. Frank and Joe rushed into the living room and found Chet standing there, looking like a drowned rat. Water dripped from his clothes onto the carpet.

"What's up?" Frank asked.

Chet's face was pale and he was panting. "The princess!" he cried. "She's been kidnapped!"

"What?" Frank demanded. "Wait. Calm down."

"This morning," Chet continued, pacing the carpet with wet sneakers, "I was supposed to pick up Salamaji at her dorm and drive her to the zoo. But when I got there, she was gone!"

"Maybe she went to the zoo without you," Joe said, turning down the volume on the TV.

"No." Chet shook his head. "I went to the zoo and was told she hadn't shown up there either. And she goes to visit Emi every single morning, rain or shine. She never misses a day."

"Maybe she had to leave town for some reason," Frank suggested. "You know, an emergency."

"I don't think so," Chet argued. "At the dorm I spoke to a friend who lives down the hall. She and

Salamaji had plans for last night. But the princess didn't keep the date, and no one at the dorm has seen her since yesterday afternoon."

"Hmmm." Frank frowned. "I don't like the sound of this."

"I already called the cops," Chet said, wiping rain from his face. "I answered a bunch of questions at the police station, but I want you guys in on this, too. We have to do something. Fast!"

"Okay," Frank said, collecting his thoughts. "Joe, change your clothes right away. Then we'll all drive out to Bayport University and see if we can find any clues there."

"I'll call Salamaji's friend," Chet offered. "She has a set of keys to Salamaji's room."

On his way out, Joe saw Aunt Gertrude hovering in the doorway to the living room. "Mercy me," Aunt Gertrude said. "A princess—kidnapped? This is more dramatic than my soap opera!"

Within minutes, Chet and Joe were driving in Chet's pickup truck, and Frank was following in the van.

"Now I'm really stumped," Joe told Chet. "The crimes keep getting more serious. First, we had the zoo sabotages, then the kidnapping of Emi, and now the kidnapping of the princess. Are these crimes connected or are they separate?"

"I don't know," Chet answered. "But I'll tell you who I think kidnapped the princess. That jerk who was following her yesterday."

"But if she thought he was dangerous," Joe countered, "why would she keep that a secret?"

"Maybe she thought he would be more dangerous if she said anything," Chet said, picking up speed. "Who knows? Maybe he threatened her."

"But what would his motive for kidnapping her be?" Joe asked, rolling down his window.

"Beats me," Chet said, making a turn. "Maybe it's a political thing. After all, she is the daughter of the king of Rashipah."

"I guess," Joe said, drumming the dashboard with his fingers. "Hey, I've been meaning to ask you something. Do you know anything about Tim Peters? He's one of the zoo's security guards."

Chet nodded. "I talked to him once. Nice guy. He's really a zoologist. In fact, he used to be one of Dr. Godfrey's assistants, but she had to let him go."

"Is that right?" Joe's eyes widened. "Dr. Godfrey mentioned she had to let an assistant go because of the funding cut. That must have been Peters!" He slapped his hand on the dashboard. "That definitely gives him a motive for sabotaging the zoo."

"But how does the princess figure into this?" Chet asked, shifting into a higher gear.

"I don't know." Joe ran a hand through his blond hair. "I just don't know."

Soon the pickup and the van drove through the campus of Bayport University and parked in front of a high-rise dormitory building. As the Hardys and

Chet headed inside, Joe brought Frank up to speed on the Peters situation.

Frank stared at Joe as he heard about Peters's being a zoologist. "Your hunch was right, Joe. We do need to check him out."

In the dorm lobby, Frank, Joe, and Chet met up with Salamaji's friend. She escorted them upstairs and loaned them the key to Salamaji's room.

"We'll return it when we're done," Chet told the girl as she headed for her own room.

Frank unlocked Salamaji's door, and the boys stepped inside a small room modestly furnished with a bed, dresser, desk, and chair. There were posters of rock groups on the wall, as well as a flag, which Frank assumed was that of Rashipah. The bed was made and everything seemed perfectly in place.

"I see no sign of a struggle," Frank said, glancing around. "If she was abducted from here, it must have been a pretty skillful job."

"Yeah," Joe said, noticing a framed picture of Emi on the desk. "Just like it was with the snow leopard."

The boys spent a few moments looking around the room, then Frank wrapped a handkerchief around his hand. "I hope the princess doesn't mind," Frank said, opening a drawer with his covered hand, "but I'm going to snoop. Maybe I'll find something relating to that boy who's been following her."

"Do you mean me?" came an accented voice.

An icy chill went up Frank's spine. He turned to see the mysterious boy from Rashipah standing in the doorway. The boy's dark eyes smoldered like embers. The stranger stepped into the room, holding something behind his back.

"What are you doing here?" Chet demanded as the boy approached.

"Easy," Frank advised his friend. They had no idea how dangerous this guy was or what was behind his back.

"I have every right to be here," the boy spoke in a tone as dark as his eyes. "The question is, what are *you* doing here?"

"You've taken the princess," Chet said, striding toward the boy. "Haven't you?"

"Stand back!" the boy demanded.

Then the boy showed what he was holding behind his back—an ivory-handled cutlass. He swung it savagely through the air.

Frank gasped as his eyes lit upon its long curved blade!

10 Over the African Plains

"You won't get away with this!" Chet rushed at the boy.

"Watch it!" the boy from Rashipah warned. He slashed the cutlass blade through the air.

In a split second, Joe reacted. He dove at the boy, tackling him to the floor. The cutlass fell with a clang and Chet quickly scooped it up.

Joe pinned the boy down in a tight wrestling hold. "Okay," he ordered, "tell us why you're here!"

"And why you're waving that weapon at us," Frank put in.

"Why are *you* here?" the boy asked defiantly. He struggled to free himself.

"The princess has been kidnapped," Chet

snapped back. "We came here to look for clues. But I bet you can tell us exactly where she is!"

The boy stopped wrestling. "Salamaji has been kidnapped?" he said with apparent alarm. *"Bahiba, mar!* I promise, I know nothing of this!"

"Then who are you and what are you doing in Salamaji's dorm?" Frank wanted to know.

"My name is Ashi-Sur," the boy said proudly. "Back in Rashipah, Salamaji was my . . . what is the word? Girlfriend. We decided to come to Bayport University together, but a month ago, she decided she did not want to be with me anymore. As you say, she broke up with me. I've been wanting to talk to her about this, but she has been avoiding me, running from me. That is why I've been following her."

"Why didn't she tell us this?" Frank demanded.

"In our country, people keep their private lives private," Ashi-Sur said, his voice tinged with scorn. "It is considered good manners. But here, people like to put their lives on television."

"You still haven't told us what *this* is about," Chet said, displaying the cutlass. "Is this good manners, too?"

Now Frank could see that the cutlass handle was a beautifully carved piece of ivory set with several gleaming jewels.

Ashi-Sur struggled to free himself again. He glared at Joe. "If you let me go, I will explain."

Joe nodded and let him sit up.

"Much better," Ashi-Sur said. He looked at

93

Chet. "The cutlass belonged to my grandfather. It is very dear to me, and I was bringing it as a gift for Salamaji. I shouldn't have threatened you with it, but you rushed at me. And . . . well, maybe I am also jealous because, for some strange reason, Salamaji seems to like you better than me."

"Why is that strange?" Chet asked. He looked wounded. "Huh? Why is that so strange?"

Frank concealed a smile.

"And what if I don't believe any of this?" Joe challenged Ashi-Sur.

"In the top drawer of the desk is a photo book," Ashi-Sur said. "Please, look at it."

Using the handkerchief, Frank pulled out a photograph album and turned through the pages, finding pictures of the princess with her family, friends, and Emi. Then Frank found several pictures of Salamaji with Ashi-Sur, their arms around each other in most of the photos.

"He's telling the truth," Frank said. "At least, I think he is."

The foreign boy stood and brushed himself off. "I must leave," he said. "I will talk to the police and see if they know where the princess might be. We should never have come to this country. The princess would still be safe."

Then Ashi-Sur snatched the jeweled cutlass from Chet and left the room.

"Can you believe she used to go out with that creep?" Chet mumbled.

"Even if he did date her," Joe argued, "he still

could have kidnapped her. In fact, it might be all the more reason. Should I go after him?"

"I think he's okay," Frank said. "Just to be sure, Chet, why don't you stay on campus and see if you can find out anything more about him. Joe, let's get to the zoo. I want to talk to Dr. Godfrey again. Especially about her ex-assistant, Tim Peters."

Back in the van, Joe took the wheel, and Frank manned the cellular phone. A few minutes later, Frank had some information.

"I just tapped into the Kellermans' phone machine," Frank reported. "Janet left a message for Jeff saying she'd meet him at a place called Carsons at six this evening. If we haven't solved the case by then, we'll pick up their trail. Put a little speed on, if you can."

Thirty minutes later the Hardys were hurrying across the wet zoo grounds. The dark clouds were now floating out of town, leaving behind humid August weather. Within minutes, Joe had found exactly who they were looking for.

"Take a look." He pointed to the kangaroo enclosure. Frank saw the gray-haired Dr. Godfrey having a heated discussion with Tim Peters.

"Let's eavesdrop," Frank suggested. The boys walked casually toward the exhibit. The enclosure was flat with patches of grass, made to resemble the scrubland of Australia. Frank and Joe pretended to watch a reddish brown kangaroo scratch at the ground as they listened to Peters and Dr. Godfrey.

95

"I made that videotape, and you have no right to keep it!" Tim Peters protested.

"But you were working for me when you made it," Dr. Godfrey argued. "Besides, I told you, I would be happy to make a copy of it for you."

"I don't want a copy!" Peters exclaimed. "I want the original. Come on, Dr. Godfrey, it's my research. Having the original could be important for my career as a scientist!"

"Oh, all right," Dr. Godfrey said, throwing her arms in the air. "If you're not going to stop pestering me, you can have it. I hid it behind the filing cabinet in the research room. Help yourself."

Just then the kangaroo came bouncing on two legs toward the Hardys as if it were riding a pogo stick. Peters turned to watch the kangaroo, then his eyes landed directly on Frank and Joe.

"Hi, Tim," Frank said, pretending to just notice him. "These kangaroos sure can hop, can't they?"

"I guess so," Peters agreed, sounding distracted. "Sorry, I can't stick around to discuss marsupials, but I have to take off." He walked away from the kangaroo enclosure at a quick pace.

"Tim, wait," Joe called, starting to follow.

"Hold on, you two," Dr. Godfrey said, glaring at the Hardys. "You two aren't 'zoo friends.' Tim tells me you're detectives. He also tells me you were wandering around the zoo last night and are probably the ones who broke into my lab. I know someone was there because my papers were out of order.

I plan to get Randy Chase to throw you out of the zoo for good."

"There goes our cover," Joe mumbled.

Guessing they didn't have much to lose, Frank threw a question at Dr. Godfrey.

"What was that videotape you and Tim were arguing about?"

"None of your business!" Godfrey shot back. "Now scram before I sick my chimps on you!"

"Like you did last night," Joe challenged.

The scientist's eyes grew large. "I don't know what you're talking about," she said. "I was home all last night."

Frank studied Dr. Godfrey a moment, trying to determine if she was being honest or not. Going on a hunch that she was, Frank decided to tip his hand. "Dr. Godfrey," he began, "we have reason to believe Tim Peters is using Wendy, John, and Michael to commit acts of sabotage at the zoo. We would very much appreciate it if you would tell us what's on that videotape he so desperately wanted."

The gamble paid off. Dr. Godfrey hesitated as a confused look crossed her face. "Using my chimps?" she echoed. She stared at Frank and Joe as she explained. "Tim used to be one of my assistants, and his research specialty was training the chimps to use human tools. He did some truly remarkable work with them, and he put most of his experiments on videotape."

Joe and Frank exchanged glances as she sighed.

"When I let him go, I rightfully kept the tape. Then yesterday he asked if he could have it back. I told him no and hid it to make sure he couldn't get to it. But just a few moments ago I gave in and told him where it was."

"I think I know why he wants that tape so badly," Joe said grimly. "Peters did the sabotage and now he's afraid that video could help prove it by showing the kind of experiments he did with the chimps. That must be why he wanted the original of the tape so badly."

"And he's probably going for it right now so he can destroy it," Frank added. "Let's go!"

The Hardys raced across the zoo grounds, and several minutes later they burst into the chimpanzee lab, finding the door partly open. The room was empty except for Wendy, John, and Michael, who were trying to build what looked like the frame of a miniature house with some lumber and their tools.

"I don't see him," Joe said, checking inside the adjoining office.

Then Frank noticed that the filing cabinet was pulled away from the wall. "He got the tape."

"We have to find him before he destroys it," Joe said. "It might be the only hard evidence we ever get on him."

Wendy started "ooh-oohing" to get Frank's attention. Frank turned and saw the chimp looking at him coyly.

"Where's Tim Peters?" Frank asked, knowing the chimp would probably understand. Wendy stuck a very human-looking hand through the bars, then John and Michael rushed over to do the same.

"They want money!" Joe cried in disbelief. "They're not going to tell you unless you pay them!"

This was no time to negotiate with a family of chimpanzees, Frank decided. He pulled out his wallet and quickly handed each chimp a dollar bill. At once, all three chimps pointed eagerly at an open window across the room.

Joe ran to the window and glimpsed Peters, far off in the distance, running.

"I see him!" Joe said, hauling himself out the window. "Come on, Frank!"

The chimps began jumping up and down and clapping as if they were watching a very exciting television show.

"You guys are the best," Frank said, waving to the chimps. "Thanks for everything!"

Frank climbed out the window and joined Joe, who was already in hot pursuit of Peters. As the brothers drew closer, running at top speed, they could see Peters was holding a black videotape case. Then Peters looked over his shoulder and caught a glimpse of the sprinting Hardys.

Immediately, Peters switched direction, and the Hardys watched him disappear into "Barambi," a mock-up of an African village. Moments later the Hardys rushed into Barambi and found themselves surrounded by a gathering of mud huts with thatched roofs. Drumbeats sounded loudly from concealed speakers, and visitors lined up at a hut that served as a fast-food concession stand.

Frank and Joe ran in and out of every hut, but they found no sign of Peters.

"Where is he?" Joe called over the maddening beat of the drums.

"There!" Frank cried, suddenly pointing. In the distance, Joe saw Peters pushing past a line of people on the boarding platform for the monorail.

By the time the Hardys reached the platform, Peters was roughly hauling several small kids out of one of the connected aqua cars of the monorail train.

"All aboard for the safari," the monorail driver called over a loudspeaker.

Peters jumped in the car just before the automatic doors slid shut. Joe saw he still had the video. Then the monorail began to move.

"Not without me!" Joe shouted, pumping his legs hard. With a powerful leap, Joe landed in a moving car occupied by two elderly couples. "Hi, there," he greeted the bewildered passengers.

"Our safari will take us over the plains of Africa," the loudspeaker announced. "Also known as the savanna. These plains are one of the best places in the world for observing animals in the wild."

As the monorail continued along its elevated track, Joe leaned over the side of his car and saw Peters alone in the next car. He was reaching into the cassette, trying to pull out the tape.

"Peters, don't destroy that tape!" Joe yelled.

"This tape is my private property!" Peters called back. "I have every right to destroy it!"

"If you'll look down," the loudspeaker reported, "you'll see a herd of zebras."

Below, Joe saw a flat grassy plain with a few umbrella-shaped trees. A herd of zebras was galloping by, their black and white stripes in motion creating a dazzling pattern.

"The zebras are quite fast," the voice on the loudspeaker continued, "which comes in handy when one of their predators is giving them chase."

Joe returned his eyes to the next car and saw that Peters had gotten some tape out.

I've got to get that cassette before he wrecks it totally, Joe thought.

"Sit down," one of the elderly women scolded.

"Actually, I'm leaving," Joe said politely.

As the lady watched in horror, Joe climbed out of the car and swung onto a fiberglass strip that connected his car to the next. He was now standing between the two cars as they moved along the track.

"You're crazy!" Peters called to Joe.

"Stop destroying the tape!" Joe called back.

"Forget it, Hardy!" Peters returned.

"We are now passing over one of the zebra's most feared predators," the loudspeaker announced. "Below you'll notice a pride of lions."

Joe reached around and grabbed on to the roof of Peters's car. Here goes nothing, he thought as he hoisted himself up and swung his feet at the car.

"Get out of here!" Peters called, standing now.

"No way!" Joe yelled, managing to work a foot inside the car.

"I mean it!" Peters shouted, giving Joe a good hard shove in the gut. Joe lost his grip. He was falling!

Joe grabbed frantically and caught on to the sliding door. He was now dangling from the monorail as it traveled over the African plains.

"Man overboard!" a passenger shouted.

"Stop the ride!" someone else yelled.

Joe glanced down, finding himself no more than two stories off the ground. Not so bad, Joe thought. If I can't pull myself up, I'll just drop down.

But Joe changed his mind when he saw the lions directly below, gazing up at him. There were several sleek beige lionesses and a single male. Everything about the male—his broad nose, his steady eyes, the majestic mane of hair circling his face—proclaimed authority.

Chet might not think the lion is king of the jungle, Joe thought, but he sure looks pretty terrifying from this angle.

The monorail screeched to a stop as Joe felt his precious grip on the door slip. His palms were sweating like crazy. He slipped again, struggling to keep his sweaty fingers on the door.

"Help!" he screamed.

Below him the male lion opened his mouth and gave a thunderous roar!

11 Dead End

Joe lifted his head and saw Peters leaning out of the car. "Help me, Tim!" Joe yelled. "I'm losing my grip."

Peters stared at him in silence.

Why should he help me? Joe thought. I'm the guy trying to put him in jail! Joe noticed other people leaning out of their cars, too far away to do anything.

Glancing down, Joe saw the male lion watching him patiently, waiting for the inevitable fall. Joe could almost feel the beast sinking its carnivorous teeth into his flesh.

Joe's sweaty hands slipped a little more.

"If nothing else," Joe called to Peters, "at least prove to me and everyone else watching that you are not a murderer!"

"Grab him!" a man yelled. "He's going to fall!"

A few very long seconds passed.

Finally, Peters reached over the side of his car and grabbed both of Joe's wrists. Joe felt himself being pulled upward until he was able to hoist himself into the car.

With great relief, Joe flopped in a seat.

"He's back in!" a passenger yelled to the front. As the other passengers cheered and clapped enthusiastically, the monorail resumed moving.

As Joe caught his breath, he looked over at Peters. The security guard picked up the video and held it on his lap, saying nothing.

"First of all," Joe told Peters, "you saved my life just now. Thanks. I mean it."

Peters merely stared into the distance.

"But you're also the one responsible for those animal escapes, aren't you?" Joe asked quietly.

As Peters nervously tapped the video with his fingers, Joe could see that only a few inches of the tape had been pulled out of the case. Joe knew neither he nor the police had a legal right to seize the tape. It belonged to Peters, and if he wanted to take it home and destroy it, he was legally free to do so.

"We are now passing over a herd of oryx," the loudspeaker reported. "They are members of the antelope family. They're also prey of the lions."

"You planned that sabotage really well," Joe said, choosing his words carefully. "And without the video, it might be tough to pin anything on you. But if people think dangerous things are still going on at the zoo, they'll just stop coming. Then the zoo takes in less money."

Peters made eye contact with Joe as he added, "I realize you may have some disagreements with the zoo board, but I know you care about the animals that live here. For their sake, let's get this thing over with."

Peters's lower lip trembled.

"Listen," Joe continued, "a few minutes ago, you proved to me that you're more good than bad. Now, tell me, please, did you commit that sabotage?"

"Yes," Peters said, briefly closing his eyes.

"What about the princess and Emi?" Joe asked. "Did you kidnap them, too?"

"The princess?" Peters looked startled at the news of her disappearance. "I didn't have anything to do with that or Emi. I have no idea where they are. Really, I don't."

"Tell me everything," Joe insisted.

"Here's the deal," Peters began. "I got my degree in zoology and was planning to make a career in chimpanzee studies. I was thrilled when I got a job as research assistant to Dr. Godfrey. These jobs are very tough to come by. I was even more thrilled when I learned she and I would be doing field research in Tanzania. It was like a dream come true."

"Then the zoo board cut the funding," Joe said.

"That's right," Peters said, removing his wire-rimmed glasses. "Suddenly, the trip was canceled, and on top of that, Dr. Godfrey had to let me go. No Africa, no job. Mr. Chase was nice enough to give me a post on the night security crew, but it isn't the same. I was devastated."

"You wanted revenge," Joe prompted.

"Yes," Peters confessed. "Then I came up with this wild plan. A way to get revenge on the zoo and at the same time put some of the work I had done with chimps and tools to practical use."

"So you taught the chimps what to do," Joe said. "Then took them out at night to arrange the three animal escapes. They cut the hot-wire, unscrewed the vents, and sawed the tree limb."

"The sabotage was really just an extension of my previous experiments," Peters said. "The stuff on the tape proves I could have gotten the chimps to do all those things, and that's why I wanted to destroy it." Peters showed a slight smile. "You know, part of me is actually proud of how I pulled off those crimes."

Joe folded his arms but didn't say anything. He had to admit Peters's scheme was clever. But endangering the zoo, as well as the animals, was just plain stupid.

"Listen," Peters went on, "I just wanted to cause some bad publicity for the zoo. I never intended for anyone to get hurt. I knew the zoo staff was well prepared for escapes and would be able to contain

106

the animals very quickly. The macaques and python were harmless, and I know tigers don't hurt humans unless they're really provoked."

"Here come the giraffes," the loudspeaker announced. "They are the tallest animals on land."

Joe watched two giraffes walk through the grass below for a moment. "I guess you were the one who set the chimps on Frank and me," he said, turning back to Peters.

"I knew you guys were snooping around the zoo for clues," Peters explained. "And then I realized Dr. Godfrey had the video and it might be damaging to me. I asked for it yesterday morning, but she wouldn't give it to me. So after I showed you around last night, I searched her office for it."

"But then we entered the lab," Joe interrupted. "When you saw us getting the chimps to saw wood, you knew we were getting wise to you. So you released the lock on the cage."

"I just wanted the chimps to scare you away," Peters said. "I was even waiting in the hall in case I needed to call the chimps off."

"Why didn't you get the tape then?" Joe asked.

"I couldn't find it," Peters said with a shrug. "Dr. Godfrey had hidden it, and it wasn't until today that she told me where it was. But . . . the truth is, Joe, in a way I'm glad you caught up with me. I'm a zoologist, not a criminal. Here."

Peters handed Joe the videocassette.

"We are now approaching the hyenas," the loudspeaker announced. "By all means, stay in your seats. Young man in the back, that means you!"

A few minutes later, the monorail returned to the platform and the doors automatically opened. A crowd was standing behind a police barrier, and four policemen were standing there. Obviously, Frank had alerted them.

"Son, you're under arrest," one of the officers said, handcuffing Peters.

Frank and Chase hurried over to Joe. "Are you all right?" Frank asked.

Joe grinned. "Don't tell me you were worried about me, just because a pride of lions was about to eat me for dinner!"

Joe then told Chase, Frank, and one of the cops everything he had learned from Peters. Joe handed the cop the video, but he also made it clear that Peters had saved his life.

"Well," Chase said, as the cops escorted Peters past the crowd, "I see the Hardys are every bit as good as their reputation."

"I'm not so sure," Frank countered. "We still have no idea what happened to Emi and Salamaji."

"When Tim said he had nothing to do with their disappearance, I believed him," Joe added. "I think he just wanted revenge."

"Let's stake out the Kellermans at Carsons," Frank said, checking his watch. "They're supposed to be there at six, but we should get there a little early."

"Do you want help?" Chase asked.

108

"Not yet," Frank said. "Let's go, Joe."

The Hardys shook hands with Chase, then walked through the zoo grounds, both of them concentrating, struggling to figure out the rest of the case.

"Are we sure the kidnapping of Salamaji and the theft of Emi are connected?" Joe asked finally.

"They must be," Frank answered. "The problem is, I don't see what the connection is yet."

Soon the Hardys came to the elephant enclosure, where they saw Hero picking up hay with her trunk and swinging it around to her mouth. As Hero began chewing the hay, a baby elephant lumbered over and butted her head against the larger elephant.

Frank watched Hero offer the baby elephant a clump of hay with her trunk. As the baby began chewing the hay, something clicked in Frank's mind.

"Hey." He nudged his brother. "See how Hero is feeding the baby."

"Yeah, so?" Joe demanded.

"Maybe it's the same with Emi and Salamaji," Frank went on. "Maybe the person who stole Emi discovered the leopard wasn't eating. Then they realized the leopard needed Salamaji, who is basically like a mother to her."

"Right!" Joe declared. "The zoo couldn't get Emi to eat until they gave her Salamaji's sari! Maybe that's the connection between the two kidnappings."

"Exactly," Frank said with a nod.

Suddenly, Chet came running up to the brothers. "I heard some maniac was dangling from the monorail," he called out. "Which of you was it?"

"Joe," Frank said with a chuckle. "Come on, Chet. Walk with us and tell us what you found."

"So far the police don't have anything on the kidnapping," Chet said as the boys walked. "I also went around campus asking questions. Ashi-Sur is a straight-A student, and he never misses a class. Someone told me he doesn't like the U.S., and someone else told me he seems sad most of the time."

"He's sad because he misses the princess," Joe commented. "Maybe enough to steal her."

"I doubt it," Frank said, checking his watch. "Chet, why don't you contact Salamaji's family in Rashipah. One of the police officers told me they already know about the kidnapping. Maybe they can give you some insight into Ashi-Sur's personality. It couldn't hurt."

"I don't see how Dr. Godfrey would have anything to do with the kidnapping," Joe mused. "Especially since we know now that Peters was working solo."

"I guess that makes the Kellermans our numero-uno suspects," Chet put in.

"But I still feel we're missing something," Frank said. "Something we know, but don't know."

The boys stopped at the polar bear enclosure, a simulation of the Arctic that was blindingly white with artificial snow. Against the white backdrop, it took Joe a moment to pick out the two pure white polar bears. Finally, their black noses gave them away.

One of the bears lumbered over to a plastic bucket and batted it playfully with its paw.

"He looks like a friendly fellow," Joe observed.

"Don't be fooled," Chet remarked. "The polar bear is the most savage animal in the entire zoo. He'd kill you just for the sport of it. He could rip your face off with one swipe of his paw."

"He's so beautiful," Joe said.

"Appearances can be deceiving," Chet reminded them. "Just like with people."

As if to prove his point, the polar bear took a ferocious chomp out of the plastic bucket.

"Come on," Joe urged. "I don't want the night to go by without our finding Emi and the princess."

At five-thirty, the Hardys drove the van toward Carsons. They found themselves in the meat-packing district on the outskirts of town. The area was empty except for trucks and several large buildings where portions of beef were stored and sold.

"There it is!" Frank pointed to one of the buildings. A sign reading Carsons hung above the doorway. The Hardys parked the van across the street from the building and climbed out.

A few minutes later, the Hardys were surprised to see Theodore Anglethorpe step out of Carsons.

The hunter with the mane of white hair had several large cardboard boxes stacked in his arms.

"What's he doing here?" Joe wondered.

"Probably buying meat," Frank guessed.

"Mind if I say hi?" Joe said.

"Why?" Frank asked.

"Maybe he'll invite us out to the island," Joe answered. "It sounds like a fabulous place."

Frank shrugged.

As Anglethorpe passed by, Joe leaned out his window. "Howdy!" he yelled.

Anglethorpe glanced around, then quickly recognized the Hardys.

"Well, hello there," Anglethorpe called to Joe. "One of my tigers is having a birthday, so I figured I'd throw a little party tonight. I just bought thirty pounds of raw steak. Now I have to get the candles and party hats!" Anglethorpe gave a boisterous laugh.

"Some folks have all the fun," Joe called, wondering if Anglethorpe was joking or really throwing a birthday celebration for a tiger. The guy sure was eccentric!

"See you later," Anglethorpe called as he walked to his car, which was parked nearby.

"Sorry, Joe," Frank consoled his brother. "Maybe he'll invite you some other time."

Anglethorpe loaded the boxes in his trunk, waved to the Hardys, then drove away. The Hardys continued sitting in their van, waiting patiently for their prey to show up.

A few minutes before six, Frank heard rock music blasting from a car radio, then he saw the Kellermans' green Chevrolet drive up and park right in front of Carsons. Jeff shut off the engine.

Frank watched the Kellermans exchange a few words, then Jeff got out of the car and went inside Carsons. Joe was about to follow him, but then he saw Janet get out of the car and move stealthily around the side of the Carsons building.

"Hey," Joe said as Janet disappeared from view. "Where is she going? It looks like she's the one who's up to something."

"For sure," Frank agreed. "I'll keep an eye on the building. Why don't you check out Janet."

Joe nodded and took off for the side of the building where Janet had gone.

Frank waited a few minutes, nervously watching the building. Joe still hadn't returned. Remembering the scare he'd got last time Joe went after the Kellermans alone, Frank finally climbed out of the van and walked to the side of the building. He noticed a strange smell and several large trash bins, but there was no sign of Joe or anyone else.

Frank crept cautiously around to the back of the building, but still there was no one in sight. What happened to Joe? Frank wondered. Frank kept going, making his way to the other side of the building.

"Frank!" Joe's voice suddenly cut through the air. "Where are you?"

Frank instantly went on alert. Following Joe's

voice, Frank raced back to the front of Carsons, where he saw Janet running for her car with Joe chasing after her.

Janet jumped into the Chevrolet, started the engine, and screeched away from the curb.

"Let's get her!" Joe cried, seeing Frank. "She ran when she saw me! She's definitely up to something!"

The Hardys dashed to the van and jumped inside.

Janet was driving away fast, obviously trying to lose the Hardys. At the end of the street, she swung into a furious turn and disappeared. Seconds later, Frank took the turn with equal fury. A few blocks down, the Hardys saw Janet's car turn again, this time into an alleyway.

The Hardys followed her into the alley, which was narrow and lined on either side by the backs of brick buildings.

"There she is," Joe said, seeing the Chevrolet a short distance ahead. The car had stopped.

"Look," Frank said, noticing that the alley led straight to a dead end. "There's no place for her to go. We've got the lady trapped."

"That's what you think!" came a voice.

Joe whipped around. Crouched in the back of the van was a man with a ponytail. It was Jeff Kellerman!

Jeff leaned forward and held the blade of a knife to Frank's throat!

12 Bitlow Island

Frank felt cold steel against his throat. By the curve of the blade, Frank figured it was a hunting knife. A very sharp one!

"Don't move," Jeff warned in a low voice. "Or I slit your throat. Got it?"

Joe glanced at Jeff, figuring out how difficult it would be to grab the knife. He inched his hand upward.

Next thing he knew, Joe felt his head being yanked backward by a rope around his neck.

"Don't try it," Janet Kellerman said, leaning into Joe's window and holding the rope.

"Try what?" Joe joked weakly.

Slowly it dawned on Joe. The last few minutes had been an elaborate trap set by the Kellermans. And the Hardys had walked right into it. Now they were in a deserted alley in a deserted part of town. No one would be stopping by to lend a hand.

"What do you want?" Frank demanded.

"Information," Jeff said. "Tell us who is in charge of your operation."

"What operation?" Joe asked, puzzled.

"Operation Alligator," Jeff answered. "We know some of it already. For example, we know illegal alligator skins are being shipped from Florida to some dealer around here. And we know this dealer is shipping them to France, where they are turned into luxurious belts and wallets and purses."

"A source in France informed us the skins were coming out of the Bayport area," Janet continued. "They gave us some shipping dates, and with a little detective work, we discovered the skins were being shipped by Specialty Express."

"Except they were being shipped in boxes from Carsons," Jeff picked up. "Your operation would buy raw meat from Carsons, then use the big airtight boxes to send the skins in. That way Specialty Express figures you're shipping smelly boxes of beef that have to be refrigerated when you're really shipping smelly alligator skins that have to be refrigerated."

"We went to Specialty Express and discovered you're planning to ship more skins tomorrow," Janet said. "Then we called Carsons, and by lining up a bunch of dates, we found the same party was planning to pick up a large order of meat today at six. And apparently that party was you."

116

"I guess you realized we were on your trail," Jeff said, increasing the knife's pressure on Frank's neck. "That's why you came by our office to check us out. Right?"

"No, you've got it wrong," Frank said. He swallowed hard, very aware he was about to be skinned himself.

"Look, we know you kids aren't in charge," Jeff said in a nicer tone. "You're probably working for your crooked uncle or something. But you're going to tell us who your boss is, and you're going to do it now. Otherwise, it's see you later, alligator!"

"I hate to break it to you," Joe said, "but my brother and I have never even met an alligator."

"It's not funny," Janet snarled, pulling the rope tighter around Joe's neck.

"Wait a second," Frank said tensely. "Please. Uh . . . look, just let us explain."

"We're waiting," Jeff said patiently.

With weapons at their throats, Frank and Joe proceeded to tell the Kellermans all about the events of the last few days. They explained how they broke into the ARF office, how they followed the Kellermans into the fur warehouse, how they tapped into the ARF phone machine, and why they had followed them to Carsons today.

"Oh, no," Janet said. She stared at her husband. "I think we went after the wrong target."

"And now it's after six thirty," Jeff said, glancing at his watch. "Carsons is closed and we probably missed the real target picking up the meat."

Both Kellermans let out a sigh of frustration.

"May I make a suggestion?" Joe offered politely.

"What's that?" Jeff asked.

"Take the knife and rope away, please."

Jeff and Janet released the Hardys. "I think we could all use some air," Frank suggested, and he, Joe, and Jeff climbed out of the van.

The Kellermans and the Hardys stood by the van, two pairs of detectives in a dead-end alley. Even though it was evening, it was still uncomfortably hot.

"You know," Frank said, wiping the sweat from his brow, "maybe all of us are looking for the same guy."

"How do you mean?" Janet wondered.

"If there is a black-market alligator dealer in the area," Frank reasoned, "he might also have interest in a snow leopard, right? After all, it is an extremely valuable animal."

"Very possibly," Jeff said, rubbing his chin. "Maybe he also deals in illegal pelts."

The cellular phone in the van beeped. Joe answered it and everyone waited, hoping a vital clue was coming through the receiver.

"That was Chet," Joe reported after the call. "He contacted Salamaji's family. They say Ashi-Sur is a little intense, but he's basically a nice guy. They seriously doubt he would kidnap the princess. Chet also checked with our friend Con Riley, at police headquarters. The cops are still as stumped as we are. I hate to say it, Frank, but it looks like we're fresh out of leads."

But Frank was busy thinking, already putting together a brand-new suspect. "You know, we did see someone at Carsons at the appointed time," he said after a moment.

"You saw a suspect?" Janet demanded.

"He showed up a little before six," Frank said, "but maybe he was the alligator trader you were tipped off about." Then Frank told the Kellermans how the Hardys had seen Theodore K. Anglethorpe coming out of Carsons with a stack of boxes.

"It's also quite possible he was just buying raw meat for his animals," Joe mentioned.

"And if Anglethorpe were involved with the animal black market," Jeff Kellerman argued, "why would he loan a snow leopard to the zoo?"

"Maybe that was just a very clever cover," Frank speculated. "The same kind of thing as using the meat container to ship the alligator skins. Maybe he was planning to steal that snow leopard from the moment Randy Chase told him Emi was coming to the zoo. And maybe he kidnapped Salamaji because Emi needed her."

"Hold on," Joe interrupted. "So far all we've got on Anglethorpe is the fact that he happened to buy some steaks an hour ago. We better be very careful before we start pointing a finger at a respected citizen like that."

"What's the name of his island?" Frank asked.

"Bitlow Island," Joe answered.

"Right," Frank said, remembering. "Anglethorpe said it was about forty miles north on the bay. Why don't we cruise out there tonight and investigate. We'll come up with some phony story why we're there. If we find something, we'll notify the authorities. If not, there's no real harm done. At this point, we don't have anything better to go on. Besides," he said, grinning at Joe, "you've been angling for an invitation to Bitlow Island ever since you met Anglethorpe."

"Okay," Joe agreed. "I'll go for that."

"As for you two," Frank said to the Kellermans, "you ought to try more peaceful tactics. Bombs and knives aren't helping your cause."

The Hardys climbed into their van, leaving the stunned couple looking after them.

"What weirdos," Joe said. "They're definitely guilty of some crimes, but not this one."

Frank started the engine and began reversing the car out of the alley. "Once we find the princess and solve this case, I plan to let Con Riley know all about the Kellermans. But for now let's call Chet and get him to meet us at the marina," Frank said, shifting gears. "We've got an excellent map on board *Sleuth,* and with some luck, we should be able to find Bitlow Island."

"I'll call Mom, too," Joe said, punching numbers on the phone. "Sounds like we'll be late for dinner."

* * *

120

Two hours later the Hardys' powerboat, *Sleuth*, was cruising through the waters of Barmet Bay. Joe was at the wheel, and Frank was next to him, holding a flashlight next to a large map of the bay. Chet was seated behind them, holding a peanut butter and jelly sandwich.

"Anybody want to finish my sandwich?" Chet asked, leaning forward.

"Uh-oh," Frank said. "Chet's not finishing his food. The guy must be really worried."

"Someone call a doctor," Joe joked.

"I'm worried about Salamaji," Chet confessed. "There's no telling what might have happened to her."

"We'll find her," Joe assured his friend.

"Veer starboard about ten degrees," Frank said, consulting the map. "By my calculations, we should be there in roughly twenty minutes."

As Joe steered the boat, the light on the prow lit the way. Otherwise, the bay was bathed in complete darkness. There was no visible moon or stars. Luckily, with his map and keen eye for landmarks, Frank managed to navigate *Sleuth* to its destination.

"That should be Bitlow Island," Frank said, peering through a set of binoculars.

A solitary island loomed ahead in the water. As the boat approached, Frank could see that the island was surrounded by a sandy beach, dotted with rocks. But the bulk of the island was so densely populated with trees, it resembled a forest.

Circling the boat around the island, Joe was

121

unable find a dock. Finally, he steered *Sleuth* into a small rocky cove. "I don't see any lights or sign of a house," he said, cutting off the outboard engine. "Where do we go?"

"The island isn't that large," Frank said, jumping off the boat onto a rock. "If Anglethorpe is here, we should be able to find him."

The boys walked up the beach, soon entering the dark fortress of trees. As Joe led the way with a flashlight, the boys trudged through the dense collection of trees and brush and undergrowth. The only signs of living creatures, animal or man, were the mosquitoes buzzing through the humid air.

"It's pretty wild here," Chet said, swatting a mosquito. "I don't even see a footpath."

"And it sure is stuffy tonight," Joe said, wiping sweat from his face. "No breeze at all."

Suddenly, the boys heard the lonely howl of a wolf in the near distance.

"We must be getting close to Anglethorpe's collection of animals," Frank said.

"Are they locked up or just roaming free?" Chet asked nervously.

"Good question," Joe said, shooting the flashlight beam through the trees. "I don't see anything—so far."

Several minutes later, the boys discovered the hunter's amazing menagerie. The trees opened into a clearing, where there stood roughly thirty large rectangular cages, each containing one or more of a certain type of animal. Most of the animals were asleep, though a few of them stirred, sensing the boys' approach.

"Look at this collection," Joe whispered in awe.

Behind the iron bars of the cages were some of the world's most magnificent creatures: red wolves, leopards, jaguars, cheetahs, ocelots, zebras, oryx, a cape buffalo, and an entire family of Bengal tigers, including a few cubs who were cuddled against their mother.

Watching two cheetahs stretched out on the ground, Frank admired how long and incredibly lean their spotted bodies were.

"That's the fastest animal on land," Chet told them in a hushed voice.

"Wow." Joe peered into a cage that contained a tiger whose coat was milky white rather than orange. "I've never seen one of these!"

"And I've never seen one of these," Frank said, moving to a cage that housed a solid white rhinoceros. The sleeping rhino was the size of a baby elephant.

A familiar, high-pitched yowl pierced the night.

"What's that?" Frank murmured.

"Sounds like a snow leopard," Joe said quietly. "Remember how the princess told us only the snow leopard howls like that?"

Frank nodded, and the boys crept toward the sound. It was coming from a cage at the far end of the animal collection.

"Look!" Chet whispered as Joe shone his flashlight into the cage.

Frank immediately recognized the smoky fur and black spots of two snow leopards. "Bingo!" he whispered.

One of the snow leopards was lying calmly on the floor, and the other was standing, watching Frank with icy green eyes. Then the second leopard slid to the ground and nuzzled its nose against something. Frank realized it was the same purple sari the princess had been wearing two days ago!

"That's Emi," Chet said quietly.

"Anglethorpe must be our man," Joe added. He quickly cut off the flashlight." The last thing we want is for him to find us here."

"Right," Frank replied. "Let's hustle back to the boat and radio the coast guard."

"But the princess . . ." Chet started. "What—"

A beam of bright light suddenly probed his face, cutting off his words.

The boys froze as the beam traveled to Frank, then to Joe.

"Don't move!" a husky voice commanded through the darkness. "We have you covered with guns."

Slowly, Joe made out the shapes of three men standing in front of them. Each of them carried a large hunting rifle that was trained on Chet and the Hardys.

"Boys." Theodore K. Anglethorpe's face suddenly loomed over the barrel of one of the rifles. "Welcome to my home."

124

"We . . . uh . . . we were just leaving," Chet fumbled.

"No." A smile slithered across the hunter's face. "I don't think you'll be going anywhere for quite some time."

13 The Game of
the Hunt

"So, Mr. Anglethorpe," Joe said casually as the hunter kept his rifle pointed at the boys. "When does the birthday party start?"

"It sounded like fun." Frank played along. "We didn't have your phone number, so we just took a chance and came on out. Hope you don't mind."

"Hey, there," Chet said, extending a friendly hand. "I'm the Hardys' best friend, Chet Morton."

"Sorry." Anglethorpe shook his head. "But you can't deceive an ol' deceiver like me. I know you boys saw that snow leopard and that purple sari. And I also know you're not stupid."

Frank quickly dropped the game. "Actually, we have been stupid," he stated. "For a while you had us thinking you were a decent guy."

"Oh, but I am," Anglethorpe said innocently.

Hearing a low growl, Frank turned to see a tan ocelot glaring at Anglethorpe. The commotion had awakened most of the animals, and they were uneasily watching the human scene being played out before them.

"Where's the princess?" Joe demanded.

"She's around," Anglethorpe answered.

"Where *exactly* is she?" Chet stepped forward.

Anglethorpe's two companions instantly cocked their rifles.

"Watch it, Chet," Joe called out as a warning. Like Anglethorpe, his men wore khakis and safari shirts. They were in their forties, one of them a white man, the other a black man. Joe could tell from their expressions they meant business.

"It's okay." Anglethorpe motioned for the men to lower their weapons. "Let's head over to the house. I'd like to chat with our . . . hmm, how shall I put it . . . our guests," he finally finished.

Anglethorpe tossed his gun on his shoulder and began trudging through the darkness. Frank, Joe, and Chet followed, and the two companions took up the rear. Behind them, Frank heard something—a wolf?—howl mournfully in its cage.

"You're an illegal alligator trader, aren't you?" Joe asked the hunter. "This afternoon you weren't picking up meat for a tiger's birthday party. You were planning to use the meat containers to ship illegal alligator skins to France."

"That's right," Anglethorpe admitted. He turned around and cocked an eyebrow at Joe,

127

seeming surprised he'd figured it out. "Been in the gator business for years," he went on.

"And what are the other animals for?" Frank asked. "Do you also sell pelts?"

"Nope," Anglethorpe said casually. "I run a sort of hunting club. You see, all of those beautiful animals back there are endangered species. Hunters come out to my island, and for a price, they can hunt the animal of their choice. If they kill it, they get to keep the head as a trophy."

Joe glanced at Frank. All of this was for sport? Anglethorpe took these animals just so he could hunt them down?

"Where do you get the animals?" Frank asked.

"I've got my connections," Anglethorpe said. "Usually, I have to bend the law to obtain them, but it's worth it. These animals are so rare and so protected by all sorts of laws that certain hunters are willing to pay a generous sum for the honor of hunting one. For example, that white rhinoceros will cost you eighty thousand dollars."

"You belong in jail," Joe declared.

"Ted, why don't we just shoot the youths?" the white companion asked in a British accent.

"That's not quite what I have in mind." Anglethorpe stopped to swat a mosquito on his neck.

Before long, the trees gave way to another clearing where a house stood. It was a handsome two-story structure built of stone, and Frank guessed it was at least a hundred years old. There was a wooden deck in front, and floodlights threw a circle of illumination around the house.

"Welcome to my humble abode," Anglethorpe said, stepping onto the deck. As Anglethorpe held open an oak door, everyone passed inside, soon entering a large den with a stone fireplace and wood paneling.

All around the room, mounted on the wall as trophies, were the heads of hunted animals. Most of the animals from the cages were represented, but the room was dominated by the enormous shaggy head of a North American bison.

Joe knew the animals' eyes were made of glass, but they still seemed to follow the humans' every move.

Anglethorpe gestured for everyone to sit, and a middle-age man and woman entered. "Jocelyn, would you bring us a pitcher of iced tea, please," Anglethorpe requested. "And, Frederick, perhaps you could turn up the air conditioning a bit."

"You stole Emi," Chet accused as everyone took a seat, "so some dumb hunter could shoot her."

"Actually, I have higher hopes for Emi," Anglethorpe said, stretching his feet on the coffee table, where a cellular phone rested. "When Randy Chase called, saying he wanted to borrow my snow leopard to breed with Emi, I got to thinking . . . Why not nab his snow leopard, see if she'll breed with mine, and then keep all the cubs myself? If it works, I'll have four or five snow leopards for my customers instead of one. At twenty-five grand apiece, that's not too shabby."

Joe looked away, disgusted. Obviously, Anglethorpe was as interested in the money as in the sport of hunting.

"Of course," Frank said, pounding his knee in frustration. "That's what I missed. The zoo had a female snow leopard, and you had a male. I should have put you on the suspect list the second Emi was missing!"

"How did you get Emi out of the zoo?" Joe asked.

"First, we caused a diversion with the birds," the black man said in a thick African accent. "Then we picked the lock on Emi's cage and tranquilized her."

"Then while all those fool security guards were chasing birds," the British man explained, "we hauled the leopard through a cut-out section of the perimeter fence. It was quite simple, really."

"But she wouldn't eat, would she?" Frank said.

"No, she wouldn't," Anglethorpe confirmed. "So I returned to the zoo the following day, and Mr. Chase mentioned that Emi needed the scent of the princess around. That's where I picked up the idea of using the sari. Remember, I saw you boys in Chase's office. Then that very afternoon, I sneaked into Salamaji's dorm room. I was in the process of swiping one of her saris when the princess herself surprised me by walking in. She knew right away what I was up to. Unfortunately, I was forced to kidnap her as well."

Frank saw Chet scowling. Like Chet, Frank was still wondering where the princess was. Is she even alive? Frank wondered.

The female servant entered, poured iced tea into glasses, and passed them around the room. Joe hated accepting the hunter's hospitality. But he took a glass because he was parched with thirst.

"How do you like my collection of heads?" Anglethorpe asked proudly. "I've hunted wild animals all over the world. From the Serengeti Plain to the polar ice caps. My two companions here are also highly accomplished hunters."

Joe caught the eye of the bison, who seemed to be rolling his glass eyes at the hunter's boasting.

"What *you* are, Mr. Anglethorpe," Chet said angrily, "is a highly accomplished liar!"

"Maybe so." Anglethorpe nodded at Chet.

"And you've got a lot of nerve calling yourself a naturalist," Joe added with contempt.

"Son, I am a naturalist," Anglethorpe claimed, after a sip of iced tea. "I believe in the natural order of the earth. And the way that natural order works is one species feeds off another species all the way up the food chain. The plant is eaten by the gazelle; the gazelle is eaten by the tiger; and so on. Not a thing in the world wrong with it."

"You are needlessly killing endangered animals," Frank argued. "How can you justify that?"

"Because man is at the absolute top of the chain," Anglethorpe said, setting down his glass. "If I need to profit from the world's animals, it is my natural right to do so. That is my firm belief."

"I thought you were rich," Joe said. "You don't even need the money."

"My grandfather who bought this island was rich," Anglethorpe explained. "And I inherited a lot of money from him. But, with my lifestyle, the money ran out pretty fast. I've always loved hunting, so I figured I'd go into the hunting business. And, of course, the alligators help, too."

Frank drained his glass of tea. "So what are you planning to do with us?" he asked.

"Ah, yes," Anglethorpe said. "I'm sorry to say, I will have to kill you. Otherwise, I would go to jail. But I've always been a sporting man."

"Congratulations," Joe scoffed.

"When hunters come to Bitlow Island," Anglethorpe continued, "they have eight hours to stalk and kill their chosen animal. If they fail to kill the animal in that time period, they still have to pay me in full. In other words, it's a game. And the animal receives a sporting chance."

"So you're going to *hunt* us?" Chet asked in disbelief.

"That's correct," Anglethorpe said. "And to prove I'm a fair man, we won't use rifles. We'll use crossbows and we'll give you a thirty-minute head start. How's that?"

"Forget it!" Joe said, standing. His blue eyes flashed with rage. "If you want to kill us, kill us! But we won't be pawns in some sicko hunting game!"

"Ignore my brother," Frank said coolly. "We'll accept your challenge. When do we start?"

"There's the spirit I expected from you Hardys." Anglethorpe checked his watch. "No time like the present," he said. "You can leave now and we won't come after you until midnight. And I'll advise you not to waste any time trying to escape from the island. We've crippled your boat, and as for swimming, I'm afraid the nearest land is thirty miles south. There's no chance you could make it."

Frank swallowed hard, then nodded. He knew Anglethorpe was telling the truth.

Anglethorpe led the boys to the front door and opened it. "Best of luck," he said as the boys stepped outside. "This should be rather interesting. I've never hunted the human species before." Then the hunter shut the door.

Frank, Joe, and Chet rushed down the deck steps and headed for the nearby trees.

Joe whirled to face his brother. "This is crazy, Frank," he exclaimed. "What're you thinking?"

Chet looked terrified. "They'll get us for sure," he added, swatting at a swarm of mosquitoes. "These guys are expert hunters and probably great trackers, and we don't have any weapons!"

"On the contrary," Frank pointed out, "we each

have a very powerful weapon. Our brains. We can beat these clodhoppers. Come on, we don't have much time. Let's put some distance between us and the house."

The boys left the glow of the floodlights and entered the dark labyrinth of trees beyond. Frank took some hope in the fact that there was plenty of natural camouflage in the trees and shrubbery.

As he followed his brother, Joe could feel his spirits lifting a little. Maybe Frank was right. Maybe they *could* beat the hunters.

"What we need is a plan," Joe stated.

"That's right, a good plan," Frank agreed.

"Okay, what is it?" Chet asked.

The boys all thought as they tramped through the damp underbrush. Frank felt a layer of sweat seeping through his T-shirt.

"In twenty-five minutes," Joe said, forming a thought, "the hunters will be leaving the house. Maybe then we can circle back to the house and call for help. I saw a cellular phone in the den."

"There's the servant couple," Chet mentioned.

"But we might be able to get past them," Frank figured. "If they don't have a gun handy."

"But the hunters might track us to the house and kill us before help comes," Chet argued.

"How about this?" Joe suggested as they walked. "We jump in the water and swim to the house. That way we'll leave fewer tracks."

"Great idea," Frank said, clapping Joe on the shoulder. "I just hope—"

Suddenly, Frank felt the ground collapse beneath his feet. He was plunging straight into the earth!

14 Pursued

Frank slammed onto a floor of dirt. Then Chet slammed down next to him. Looking up, Frank realized he and Chet had fallen into a pit about nine feet deep, the top camouflaged with leafy tree limbs.

Above them, Joe was clinging desperately to the upper rim of the pit.

"Pull yourself up, Joe," Frank called. "If *you* fall, we're all stuck down here!"

"Doing my best," Joe grunted He strained to pull his body upward. Finally, achieving something like a chin-up, Joe managed to hoist himself out of the pit and onto solid ground.

He stared down at the pit in amazement.

"I guess it's a trap for animals," he said, catching his breath. "Something to help the hunters get their prey. As if their weapons aren't enough. Hold on," he added. "I'll get you out of there."

Joe dropped to his stomach and extended his arm. With some effort, he pulled Frank back up to the surface.

Together, Frank and Joe reached down for Chet.

"Bet you wish I didn't weigh so much," Chet joked as the brothers struggled to pull their husky buddy upward. But nobody laughed at Chet's weak joke. The fall into the pit had made them lose precious time, time that they all knew they couldn't afford to lose.

Finally Chet was back on solid ground.

"It's midnight," Joe said, checking his watch. "The three ghouls should be leaving the house right about now. Let's head for the water."

"I've made an improvement on the plan," Frank said. "You guys go to the house without me."

"Without you?!" Chet exclaimed. "Why?"

"Shhh," Frank urged. "It will help if one of us acts as bait. If I'm out here leaving tracks, that will keep the hunters busy and give you guys a better chance of making it safely to the house."

"Forget it," Joe protested. "I'm not leaving you out here alone!"

"Yes, you are," Frank said evenly. "It's the best way. I'll be okay and so will you. Get a move on."

"Well . . . okay." Finally, Joe gave in. He didn't want to, but he knew Frank was right. Creating a kind of bait was a good idea. He just had to act as if everything would turn out okay.

"Good luck, little brother," Frank said, flashing a reassuring smile.

"Same to you." Joe punched Frank lightly on the shoulder.

Without another word, Joe and Chet walked away, soon disappearing behind a tangle of trees.

Suddenly, Frank felt very alone. He knew his strategy would be helpful to Joe and Chet, but he also knew he was in real danger now. Three armed hunters were coming after him and he had nothing to fight them with except his own wits. Yes, he would have to be extremely smart tonight.

Frank listened very intently, but there was nothing but the eerie silence of Bitlow Island. He focused his hearing as if he were tuning in a weak radio station. Soon he detected voices in the distance.

Instantly, Frank felt his heartbeat triple in tempo. The game was starting and the stakes were life and death. Moments later the voices grew a little closer and a little clearer.

"The tracks are easy to follow," Frank heard one of the men say. "It looks like they headed straight for one of the pit traps."

"They probably fell right in." The British man chuckled. "Foolish youths."

Desperately, Frank wondered what to do. Climb a tree and wait for them to pass by?

But then if they find me in the tree, Frank thought, I'll be a sitting duck.

"If we find they've split up, we should split up, too," Anglethorpe said.

Frank moved lightly across the ground. Maybe if I just keep in motion, Frank figured, I can stay alive until Joe and Chet phone the coast guard.

Watch the ground, Frank reminded himself. Falling into another pit could be a fatal mistake.

"They *did* fall in the pit," Frank heard the African say. "At least two of them did."

Frank realized he was being pursued by top-notch trackers. For them, catching up with him would be a piece of cake. As Frank continued moving through the maze of trees, he sensed how a wild animal must feel when a predator was stalking it across the plains or desert or swamps or jungle or anything. Terrified and desperate.

"This way," Frank heard the African say.

They are *right on my trail*, Frank thought. I need a trick up my sleeve and I need it fast.

Suddenly, a high-pitched yowl pierced the night.

I feel the same way, Emi, Frank thought.

Then an idea seized Frank. The animals!

Frank heard another yowl and shifted direction. He trotted toward the sound of one snow leopard's distinctive calls. He would set some of the animals free, creating a distraction and a danger to the hunters. It might buy him enough time to stay alive until help arrived.

Before long, Frank came to the community of animal cages. Some of the animals were awake, peering at Frank through the bars of their cages. Frank knew the animals he set free could also be dangerous to him, but it was a necessary risk.

Frank pulled a metal pick from his cutoffs and began picking the padlock on the snow leopard cage. Frank noticed a bloody bone in the cage and hoped the leopards had been fed enough meat for dinner. Maybe they're too full to be interested in more food, he thought.

A moment later, Frank eased the cage door open.

Frank stood very still as the two snow leopards ambled slowly out of the cage. They both began sniffing the ground with deep curiosity.

"Yes," Frank said softly, "it's nice to be out of there, isn't it?"

Suddenly, the two snow leopards bounded off through the trees for a midnight run of the island.

Frank had to hold back a triumphant shout. It looked as if the animals were more interested in freedom than in attacking him. All he could do was hope that some of the animals would be less friendly to the men who had been holding them prisoners.

Next, Frank approached the cage of the white tiger. The exquisite white feline stared at Frank with pale blue eyes that resembled sapphires.

"Hi, beautiful," Frank said as soothingly as possible. "I met a cousin of yours the other day."

Frank inserted his pick in the padlock.

* * *

About ten minutes later, Joe and Chet pulled themselves out of the bay and clung to a rock.

"I think we're pretty near the house," Joe said, brushing back his wet hair. "Do you need a rest? We were swimming against the current there."

"Just a second," Chet said, breathing hard.

Suddenly, the boys heard a terrifying human scream that came from the far side of the island. The next second they heard nothing but the water lapping gently against the rocks.

Chet and Joe locked eyes.

"Was that Frank?" Chet whispered after a moment.

"I don't know," Joe admitted. "I guess . . . I guess it could have been."

"Come on, let's head for the house," Chet urged. "I'm sure Frank's okay. I'm sure of it."

Joe and Chet scrambled across rocks on the beach, trying not to leave a single track. Then they entered the dark shroud of trees. They moved through the dense trees and brush as fast as possible—a tough job now that they were sopping wet and barefoot.

Before long, the boys came to Anglethorpe's house and climbed quietly onto the deck. Peering into a window, Joe saw the servant couple in the den, watching television. On the coffee table was an automatic pistol and a cellular telephone.

"The phone is good news," Chet whispered. "But the pistol isn't."

Joe's eyes shifted to the big shaggy bison mounted on the wall. For a moment, it seemed that the bison was sending Joe a message: *Don't let these hunters get you, too, kid.*

"Let's check around back," Chet suggested. "Maybe there's a window we can sneak through. There's bound to be another phone in the house."

The boys made their way around to the rear of the house. There were several windows on the ground floor, but each was securely locked.

"We could smash our way in," Joe figured, "but the noise would draw the guy with the gun. Too risky."

Chet glanced up at several dark windows on the second floor. "I bet the princess is up there."

"Maybe she can pull a Rapunzel and let down her hair for us," Joe cracked, grimly. Then he noticed a storage shed a short distance behind the house. "Hey, maybe there's something in there we can use."

The boys crept to the shed and found it secured with a padlock. Joe pulled the metal pick from his pocket and quickly managed to undo the lock. Then Joe slid back an iron bar, opened the door, and stepped inside the pitch-dark shed.

At once, something grabbed Joe from behind, and he felt teeth tear into his wrist. "Chet!" Joe called. "Watch out!" He jerked away, crashing into a metal cage.

"What?" Chet whispered, entering the shed.

"Chet? Joe?" someone else whispered.

As a dim light flipped on, Joe saw Salamaji standing there holding a camping lantern. Her clothes and black hair were rumpled, but otherwise she seemed alive and well.

"I am so happy to see you," Salamaji murmured. "I am sorry I bit you, Joe. I thought you were one of my captors. This is where they have been keeping me."

"Are you all right?" Chet asked with concern.

"Yes," Salamaji said. "For the most part."

"I'm awfully glad to see you," Chet said.

At that, Salamaji sobbed and fell into Chet's arms.

"All right, you two," Joe said, taking the lantern from Salamaji. "Stand outside, away from the flood-lights, and make sure no one comes while I look around in here. And be very quiet."

After Chet and Salamaji left the shed, Joe closed the door and began searching for anything that might be useful. There was a sleeping bag on the floor along with spare cages and maintenance supplies. In a hidden compartment, Joe found a box of tranquilizer darts, similar to the ones used the other day on the Bengal tiger. He also found a copper tube to shoot them with. Anglethorpe must have forgotten about the darts, Joe thought. No way would he have locked up the princess in the shed if he'd remembered them.

"Aaaaah!" Chet yelled from outside.

Joe's heart skipped a beat.

Cracking open the shed door, Joe saw Chet

143

backed up against a tree, his eyes wide with fear. Salamaji was standing beside Chet, a hand clutched over her mouth in horror!

Joe cracked the door farther open, seeing nothing but the darkness and the surrounding trees. Then he spotted one of the hunters. The man held a wooden crossbow, a weapon similar to, but smaller than, a regular bow. He was holding the bow in the horizontal shooting position, and Joe noticed it was loaded with a feather-tipped arrow.

"That was very clever of you to swim to the house," the man said with a devious smile. "But I followed your footsteps to the water and figured that was what you were up to. You see, a good tracker not only follows the prey, he *thinks* like the prey. And now I have to kill the prey."

He lifted the crossbow to eye level and took careful aim at Chet's heart. Then he skillfully pulled back the bow string.

Oh, no, Joe thought. Chet has only a second left to live!

15 Survival of the Fittest

Joe heaved the lantern with all his strength at the hunter.

Seeing the hurtling streak of light coming at him, the man ducked. The lantern crashed to the ground and instantly went out.

Chet dashed from the tree, but the man followed him with the crossbow and released the bow string. The arrow whizzed by Chet, landing in the trunk of another tree. Swiftly, the man pulled another arrow from his quiver. As he loaded his bow, Salamaji lunged for his hand and bit it fiercely.

"Ahhh!" the man yelled, dropping the arrow.

The next second, Chet plowed into the hunter, knocking him to the ground.

By this time, Joe had fetched the copper tube and loaded it with a tranquilizer dart. He put the tube to his lips, aimed, blew hard, and sent a tassled dart straight into the black man's arm. Chet put his hand over his captive's mouth and kept it there until, moments later, the man fell unconscious. Using a coil of rope found in the shed, Joe and Chet tied the hunter securely to a tree.

"One down," Joe said.

Hearing the front door of the house open, Joe, Chet, and Salamaji rushed to duck behind a clump of trees. Joe could see the male servant standing on the porch with his gun, scanning the area.

"Can you nail him with the crossbow?" Chet whispered.

"I doubt it," Joe whispered back. "And if I miss, he comes after us with the pistol. But we do need to get to that cellular phone somehow."

"There's a boathouse across the island," Salamaji whispered. "I believe I can find it. If we can break into it, the boats have radios."

Joe nodded, picked up the copper tube, and handed Chet the box of darts. The threesome crept quietly away from the house, then soon they all broke into a sprint. As he ran, Joe felt the twigs and brush tearing into his bare feet, and after several minutes, his body was slippery with sweat.

"It's not much farther," Salamaji panted.

"Good." Chet gasped.

"Whoa," Joe said, suddenly stopping. A few steps ahead, a jaguar with a tan coat and black splotches was sniffing at something on the ground. "Where did he come from?" Joe whispered.

"I don't know," Chet said. "But keep still. These animals are probably meaner than zoo animals because they're not treated or fed as well."

"What's he sniffing?" Salamaji wondered.

Then Joe felt all the blood rushing out of his head. The jaguar was sniffing a strip of what appeared to be Frank's T-shirt, and the cloth was stained with fresh blood!

"No!" Joe yelled.

"Shhh!" Chet urged. "Stay calm!"

But it was too late. The jaguar turned its green eyes to Joe and unleashed a ferocious roar!

Before Joe could react, the wild animal pounced on him and knocked him into the dirt. Joe felt claws at his shoulder and a blast of hot breath in his face. As he faced the jaguar, he could also see its bared teeth.

With all his might, Joe grabbed the animal's head and struggled to hold it away. The jaguar growled fiercely as Joe saw Chet diving at the cat with a tassled dart. The jaguar wrestled violently in Joe's arms several moments, then collapsed on top of him.

"Ugh," Joe groaned. "This guy's heavy. Give me a hand, Chet."

With Chet's help, Joe shoved the limp jaguar off him. Then he checked the streaks of blood on his shoulder. The jaguar had managed to scratch him, but that was all.

"Let's hurry," Joe said, jumping up and retrieving the fallen tube. "Frank may be in worse shape than I am!"

Joe, Chet, and Salamaji tore across the island. Soon they came to a rocky ridge that overlooked a stretch of open beach.

"The boathouse is somewhere along this beach," Salamaji explained. One by one, Joe, Chet, and Salamaji climbed down the steep rocks and began hurrying along the sandy shoreline.

"I think we're close," Salamaji assured her friends after they traveled a distance through the sand.

"Well, hello there!" someone called.

Joe looked up. Anglethorpe stood on the rocks overhead, his crossbow aimed right at Joe.

"It won't help you to run," Anglethorpe called. "You're completely exposed, and I'm an awfully good shot."

Joe glanced around. He quickly realized that Anglethorpe could easily kill him before he reached either the water or the nearby rocks. Chet and Salamaji stood helplessly alongside Joe.

"Drop that copper tube!" Anglethorpe ordered. Having no choice, Joe dropped the tube onto the beach.

"Congratulations, Joe," Anglethorpe called. "At least it took longer to find you than your brother."

Frank! Joe could feel his heart pumping. "What happened to him?" he demanded.

"He tried to get smart," the hunter said. "He released some of the animals, I guess figuring it would make things tougher for us. But instead they ate him alive. I followed his tracks, but all I found were some strips of his bloody shirt. So I left his trail and went after you. I see you have the princess with you. Hello, Your Royal Highness."

"*Bahibah comina!*" Salamaji shouted to the sky.

"What's that you said?" Anglethorpe asked. "I'm afraid I don't speak your language."

"She probably said, 'You're a monster!'" Joe roared with anger. "Because that's what you are!"

"Have you ever heard the term 'survival of the fittest'?" the hunter roared back. "That's the way the evolution of a species works. Now then, kids, I am bigger and smarter and stronger than you are, and therefore you are going to die!"

"If anybody dies, Anglethorpe"—a voice tore through the darkness—"it's you!"

Joe wanted to cheer. He'd know that voice anywhere. He stared hard into the trees beyond the rocky ridge and finally glimpsed Frank perched high on a tree limb. By now, Frank looked something like a wild animal himself. Frank was shirtless, and most of his body was scratched and smeared with dirt. Joe also noticed Frank had a crossbow aimed directly at Anglethorpe.

"I knew he was okay!" Chet whispered. "Frank would never let this dude outsmart him."

"Nobody ate me alive, Anglethorpe," Frank boasted. "After I freed the animals, I climbed a tree. Then, in the distance, I heard one of the cats attacking your British friend. He screamed and I

149

think he jumped into one of those pit traps to escape the cat. He's probably still there, cowering in fear!"

Joe now knew who'd screamed earlier. The Brit.

Joe glanced sideways at Salamaji. The princess had lost it. She was staring out into the darkness, crying out words in her native tongue.

"Bahibah comina!" Salamaji shouted again.

"Then something that happened the other day gave me an idea," Frank continued. "When I heard you closing in on me, Anglethorpe, I tore up my shirt and rubbed it with some bloody bones I found in one of the cages. You thought I was dead and walked right by me. If I was a snake, I'd have bit you. Then later I heard Joe yell and I ran in that direction to find him. Along the way, I stumbled on the Brit's crossbow."

"Abdati!" Salamaji screamed.

"What are you hollering about?" Anglethorpe asked, keeping his crossbow trained on Joe.

Salamaji looked startled. "I am saying my prayers," she confessed. "It looks like I may be killed very soon."

"True," Anglethorpe replied. "Although I do have to compliment you kids. You've all proved yourselves to be quite brave tonight. I'm almost sorry I have to take you down."

"I'll take you down first!" Frank called from the tree. "I'm pretty handy with a crossbow."

Anglethorpe's large body shook with laughter. "Don't lie to me, son. You've probably never shot a

150

crossbow in your life. It takes years to master. I'll bet you anything I can kill all four of you before Frank lands a single arrow. Let's see. The first arrow goes to Joe Hardy."

Lifting the crossbow to his eyes, Anglethorpe took a deadly aim on Joe.

Frank sprang into action, relying on his every instinct. He knew Anglethorpe was right. There was maybe one chance in a hundred he would hit his target.

Meanwhile, down on the beach, Joe closed his eyes. *Now I know how that bison on Anglethorpe's wall felt,* Joe thought. *I'm trapped.* It would take a miracle to save him now.

Frank and Anglethorpe both eased back their taut bowstrings—farther, farther, farther. . . .

"Emi, sabu!" Salamaji screamed. Now she was pointing at Anglethorpe.

Appearing out of nowhere, Emi sprang off a rock and lunged at Anglethorpe's massive body. On impact, the hunter and snow leopard both fell to the beach below, the hunter rolling in the sand. Emi kept her balance and, with a loud yowl, opened her jaws to take a savage bite out of the man.

"Emi, banta!" Salamaji commanded.

Emi took a step back, her midsection heaving. Anglethorpe tried to make a break for it, but Joe approached him with the copper tube in his mouth. Joe blew, and a tranquilizer dart went zooming into Anglethorpe's leg.

"Owww!" Anglethorpe screamed, clutching at the dart. Chet and the princess ran over, and the snow leopard turned to Salamaji, her tongue panting, as if to ask, *Now what should I do?*

"*Nabi,*" Salamaji said, wrapping her arms around the snow leopard's neck.

As Anglethorpe lay in the sand, Frank jumped off a rock down to the beach.

"Guess I was wrong," Anglethorpe said. His speech was slurred from the effect of the tranquilizer drug. "You folks are . . . surviv . . . maybe we can . . . work some deal—"

The hunter's head slumped into the sand.

"You weren't saying your prayers, were you?" Chet asked the princess. "You were calling Emi!"

"When I saw the jaguar, I realized Emi might also be roaming around," Salamaji said, stroking the leopard's spotted back. "If she were free, I knew she would come if I called her."

"Let's find that boathouse and radio the coast guard," Joe suggested. "Maybe they'll put Mr. Anglethorpe where he belongs. In a cage."

Five nights later the Hardys were back at the Bayport Zoo, this time attending a fund-raising ball. As a band played in Zoo Plaza, multicolored lights twinkled from the trees and well-dressed guests danced their way around the seal fountain.

Frank and Joe were dancing with their girlfriends, Callie and Iola, and Chet was dancing with his date, Salamaji, the princess of Rashipah. When the band stopped playing for a short while, the boys and their dates headed for the sidelines.

"Having a good time?" Randy Chase asked as he strolled up to the group. Frank noticed a snow leopard painted on the zoo director's necktie.

"Yeah, great bash," Joe said, his arm around Iola. "How are the new boarders doing?"

"They're all doing wonderfully," Chase said, sounding like a proud father. The Bayport Zoo had taken in all of the animals from Bitlow Island, while the Bayport jail had welcomed Theodore K. Anglethorpe and his companion hunters.

"Look who's joining the party," Frank said.

Joe turned to see Dr. Sara Godfrey walking to the refreshment table. Following behind, as if they were in a parade, were Wendy, John, and Michael, each wearing a colored party hat. As the chimps passed by, John and Michael waved to the Hardys, and Wendy made the hand signs for "zoo friends."

"Do you mind if I visit Emi?" Salamaji asked the group.

"We'll all go with you," Chet suggested.

The animals were being kept in their daytime habitats for a while tonight so that the ball-goers could visit them.

When the group arrived at the snowy Himalayan mountainside, Emi was nestled up against the snow leopard from Bitlow Island. Emi was fondly licking the other leopard's smoky-colored coat.

"How do you like that?" Frank told the princess. "Emi doesn't even notice you're here."

Salamaji grinned. "I think she has found some-one she likes even better."

"It's like a love story," Callie agreed. "They look so happy together."

Frank and Joe groaned as the girls continued to coo over the contented cats.

"Okay, enough romance," Joe announced finally. "Let's head back to the dance and grab some more grub before it's all gone. I'm still hungry."

"Good idea," Frank agreed.

"Here, here," Chet cheered. "You know I'm always up for a snack!"

"Boys," Salamaji said with a deep sigh. "They are so . . . what is the word?"

"*Beastly?*" Callie wondered.

"Exactly!" Salamaji said.